Bannerman, Mark

Blind trail /
Mark Bannerman

LP

BLIND TRAIL

Whilst on military patrol for the United States Cavalry, Lieutenant Raoul Webster is blinded in a freak accident. Guided by his young brother, he sets out for San Francisco to consult an eye doctor. But, en route, their stagecoach is ambushed by ruthless Mexican bandits. Raoul's brother is murdered, as are the driver and all the male passengers. Raoul survives, but he is alone in the wilderness and vulnerable to all Fate can throw at him. He is kept alive by one burning ambition, to track down his brother's killer . . .

MARK BANNERMAN

BLIND TRAIL

Complete and Unabridged

LINFORD
Leicester

First published in Great Britain in 2004 by
Robert Hale Limited
London

First Linford Edition
published 2005
by arrangement with
Robert Hale Limited
London

Bannerman, Mark
    Blind trail.—Large print ed.—
Linford western library
1. Western stories
2. Large type books
I. Title
823.9'14 [F]

ISBN 1–84395–838–4

Published by
F. A. Thorpe (Publishing)
Anstey, Leicestershire

Set by Words & Graphics Ltd.
Anstey, Leicestershire
Printed and bound in Great Britain by
T. J. International Ltd., Padstow, Cornwall

This book is printed on acid-free paper

*Dedicated to all those who bravely
contend with impaired vision*

1

She laughs only rarely, though when she does, the sound comes sweetly, like spring rain sliding over pebbles. I guess her age is late teens. All too soon she becomes serious again and lapses back into her soft Louisiana drawl, but try as I do, I cannot catch what she is saying. The relentless rattle of the coach, the grind of wheels and axles, is too loud.

I am sitting tightly wedged against my brother. I place my mouth close to his ear and ask, 'James, is she pretty?'

I hear him laugh shyly and he says, 'Yes, Raoul, she is pretty. Her hair . . . it's as black as jet.'

The heat of Arizona Territory is stifling; our clothing is moist with sweat. It is a dry, sucking heat that, given the chance, will scorch the skin. Borne on gusty wind is the pungent, bittersweet odour of sage. The canvas side-curtains of the coach are pinned down, yet the dust still wafts in and feels gritty as powdered glass between the teeth. We are in canyon country. It is a world, my brother tells me, of scorpions, spiny cactus, bladderweed and mesquite.

It is also a world where a terrible fate awaits us.

A half-hour back, James mentioned how the trail ran along the side of a steep mountain, little more than a narrow shelf, with a thousand-foot precipice on one side, but, being blind, I was spared the apprehension that such views bring. Blind trust has its compensations. Now, as we swing around curves and jolt over potholes and stones, we are bounced about inside, for the seats lack the benefit of springs, and the coach jumps up and down on its leather thoroughbraces, jarring our bones beyond belief. Drivers, or 'knights of the rein' as they are sometimes called, are determined to maintain schedules regardless of hazard and discomfort. Our current driver is taking full advantage of the reckless spirit of the four California horses that draw us and seem anxious to escape their traces in headstrong gallop. I long to soak in a cool bath but realize we will experience little luxury until we reach San Francisco — and that is a week away.

'The trail is so narrow,' James confides, 'I could touch the rocky side if I reached out.'

I know that the way is narrow. I have heard mesquite scraping the coach's sides.

'The narrowness doesn't slow us down,' I say, and am obliged to repeat my words more loudly so as to be heard above the roar of wheels. 'Do you regret you chose to come this way instead of travelling by rail?'

Again his young laugh comes. 'Never! I'm glad I talked Father in to letting us travel by stage. One day soon, the West will no longer be wild. Civilization will trample over it and it will be gone for ever. We must enjoy it while we have the chance.'

'How much longer to the next way station?' I enquire.

'About two hours, Raoul, but we shall stop before then. And I'm loving every moment of this journey.'

He is eighteen, five years younger than me. His energy and enthusiasm are boundless.

I feel that unless I consciously embrace each bump, my stomach will end up in my mouth. I shift my position slightly, trying to find greater comfort, but it is difficult because there are several valises wedged against our legs. James has told me how the rooftop and rear-end boot are nigh overflowing with sacks of mail.

I wonder if the girl is discomforted. Amid all her talking, I am sure she does not complain.

Locked in my dark world, I try to sleep, but I am not tired, so I let my mind drift back to when I gained my cadetship to the Military Academy,

West Point, in 1878, and gave my word before God to uphold the Union. I thus followed in the footsteps of my father who had attained the rank of brigadier-general and served with distinction in the Civil War. I enjoyed the study of philosophy, mathematics, French and Spanish, but not as greatly as lessons in leadership, weaponry and military tactics. Fearing failure above all else, I strove my utmost to be a model cadet, studying hard in those gloomy class-rooms that over-looked the tree-lined Hudson River. In 1882 I took my final examinations and graduated, third in my class of twenty, with special commendation for horsemanship. In New York I purchased my sword, sidearm and spurs, and posed in my lieutenant's stars and yellow-piped trousers for ambrotype, my boots polished like black anthracite, my face filled with naïveté and the irresponsibility of boyish dreams. Within a month, I was assigned to the United States 3rd Cavalry.

It was a year later, in Colorado, while leading my troop on patrol, that a corporal discharged his carbine in error. The ball struck me across the forehead. I remember nothing of subsequent events, until I regained consciousness in the post hospital at Fort Stanton and a doctor explained to me what had happened.

'Doctor,' I said, 'I cannot see. When can I have the bandage taken from my eyes?'

His next words have haunted me to this day. 'Raoul, there is no bandage over your eyes. You are lucky to be alive. If the bullet had gone an inch closer, you'd be dead. The gods are on your side. They must have decided your time's not up.'

The Army was generous, thanks to my father's influence. Discarding my uniform, I was given extended furlough during which to attempt the recovery of my sight. I suffered leeches, blistering, purgatives and electric shock to the eyeballs that left suppuration streaming down my cheeks, but all to no avail. Subsequently, my father corresponded with Professor Otto Rattner in San Francisco, a German physician who has achieved considerable renown in treating blindness with the use of somewhat controversial practices. He agreed to examine me. I am filled with optimism. Needless to say, I can scarcely wait for this journey's end so that the good professor can enable me to restore my uniform, resume my career and again enjoy life to the full.

My brother James has an adventurous nature and would have delighted to follow me into the Army, but sadly he was blighted by a leg crippled at birth and thus prevented, as he grew up, in tackling the more physical activities. Instead, his intention is to be apprenticed into law. But he nurtures an abounding interest in the Western frontier and was thrilled at the prospect of conducting me to San Francisco, seeing the journey as his opportunity to experience the wilderness before it is obliterated by so called 'Manifest Destiny'.

In the meantime there seems little for me to do but listen for the black-haired girl's occasional laughter, imagine her prettiness and strain to catch her Louisiana words. I am sure she refers to her companion as 'Uncle', but further comprehension is prevented by the racket of our progress. I can smell the rich aroma of his cigar rising above the taint of sweat which is prevalent in us all.

Twenty minutes later the brakes screech and the coach complains furiously at being compelled to stop. Once the driver has won his battle, the door is thrown open and we dismount, stamping the stiffness from our legs, feeling like sea passengers coming ashore after a month on turbulent seas. James leads me up a slope into some trees that scent the air with the fragrance of balsam. Here we undertake our toilet, after which we walk down-slope, kneel amid the stiff bristles of wire grass and refresh ourselves in a cool stream. It is only inches deep. Close by, I can hear the girl and her uncle. Our ears have adjusted to the sweetness of natural sounds, the twittering of jays, and the buzz of dragonflies and gnats.

It is then that a strange Mexican voice slashes like a sabre across the tranquillity.

'Ever'body, put your hands up!'

* * *

The menace is so clear, so deadly, and awakes a single, shrill cry of fear from the girl. For a moment, I am unconscious of any sound, apart from the frightened pant of breathing. Then, into that stunned silence, comes something new — the metallic clink of bullets sliding into the breeches of rifles, the snapping of bolts, and not just from one direction. We seem surrounded.

In my mind, I form a tableau of the scene. James and I are crouched by the

9

stream, poised like statues, our mouths agape with shock. A yard or so along the bank are the girl and her uncle, standing petrified. Attending the still-harnessed horses, the driver and guard have stopped their work, frozen into inactivity. And framing the tableau, like shark's teeth, an unwavering torque of aimed rifles, numbering anything between six and a hundred, I have no means of determining.

'Ever'body, hands up or you die — now!'

The repeated order comes with frightening finality, offering no margin for further hesitation. My own hands are moving up and I can only assume the others are also complying — but no.

The blast of a carbine smashes into the tenseness, coming not from our molesters, but from the direction of the coach, and it frightens me not only for what it precedes but because it reminds me of the shot that blinded me. It is followed by the spiteful, rapid fire of a handgun.

I feel James's hand claw at my coat, dragging me earthward, his hissed words breathed into my ear. 'Get down, get down! The guard and driver have opened up!'

There is no more talk. We hug the ground as the air seems to erupt about us with the whine of lead and the thunder of retaliatory gunfire. Oh, for my eyes and a pistol in my hand! But I can do nothing but cower, feel the fearful tremble in my body, and submit to Fate. The intensity of fire increases. I can hear bullets splintering the bark of trees, spouting up the stream's water, striking the bank, throwing up chips of rock, seeking out our vulnerability. And now, to my utter horror, James utters a cry and when I scream his name, he does not answer. I reach out, clutch onto his sleeve. He moves slightly. He is groaning — a thick, gurgling sound, deep in his throat — and I shout with dismay.

In retrospect, it will be easy to blame the stupidity of the coach's driver and guard for opening fire on the men who threatened us. Perhaps they did not appreciate the degree to which we were outnumbered. They did nothing but bring death down upon themselves and others.

But now, all my handicapped senses can convey is the scream of men as they are hit, the shudder of the ground about me being raked by bullets, the roar of gunfire rising through a crescendo to all embracing, deafening noise, on and on and on, until finally it is pierced by the shouting of Mexican voices. Only then do the guns fall silent.

The silence hurts my ears, for it is not true silence, but a blanket that muffles lesser sounds — the groans of the dying, the renewed, now hushed, murmur of the Mexicans, the nervous, wheezy blowing of a horse, the incongruous gurgling of the stream over the rocks. I have no doubt that the other passengers, the girl and her uncle, are dead or dying, as are the driver and guard.

Suddenly stones are escaping noisily from beneath heavy boots, and a man is leaning over me. I can smell his pulque-tainted breath, his sweat, his urine-tainted clothing.

'This one still lives!'

There are more footsteps. Another man has approached from behind.

'Jesus! Kill him,' he says. 'All the others are dead now.'

The hammer of a pistol is thumbed back. The hard muzzle of the gun presses against my head. It is hot from recent fire; I feel it is branding a ring into my temple.

In my nightmare world, I have forgotten my brother and the sad condition he must be in. But he has not forgotten me. His voice is little more than a guggling whisper, driven from lungs that are already flooded with blood, yet it comes with a desperate insistence, speaking the last sentiment he is ever to express.

'Do not harm him. He is blind!'

The gun is withdrawn from my head,

as if its holder seeks to gain better purchase on the trigger, or, dare I imagine, it is out of compassion, even mercy?

Then the weapon explodes.

2

The taint of blood thickens the air. It draws flies. I can tell by the loudness of their drone that they are big. Each drone rises in volume, impatient and angry, coming from hither and thither, then suddenly stops, and I realize that its initiator has settled upon some gory segment of flesh, its mandibles sucking greedily. When it is gorged, its bloated heaviness will render flight difficult. Sometimes I feel flies upon me, but I brush them away. I run my fingers across my face and scalp. I probe into the sightless sockets of my eyes, my nostrils, lips. My face is not bleeding. I lick my fingers and know it is sweat that makes it seem so moist. The air has cooled. The afternoon has stretched into evening. Perhaps I have slept. Perhaps the whole horrific affair has been a dream, a petrifying fantasy that has no roots in reality, but my memory and awareness cling to me like limpets to a ship's hull, will not relent.

If only I could see.

I reach out. My fingers claw onto the sleeve of a coat, and then the arm inside. It is lifeless. It is my brother's. Anger floods through every vein in my body, has me grinding my teeth and sobbing aloud. Why? Why James who was so full of life and adventure and battled so bravely with his crippled leg? I recall his last words: *Do not harm him. He is blind*. His was no grovelling plea for his own life. His thoughts were only for me — and so the bullet previously intended to expel my brains was turned on him. Yes, sweat moistens my face — and tears, for my eyes have not been robbed of their ability to weep.

I hear a flapping sound. At first it puzzles me, but then I hear a raucous, quarrelsome squawking and realization seeps into my brain. Buzzards, turkey-vultures, have been drawn from on high, drawn by their uncanny sensing of carrion. Can its stench, still comparatively fresh, taint the thermals a thousand feet up, or do their eyes possess telescopic powers to pin-point their next meal? And why is it that they appear to hunt alone, yet the presence of carrion attracts them in droves? Their mewing cries are mournful, synonymous with death.

Suddenly I hate them. I imagine their beaks drawing bloody sinews from the bodies strewn about, perhaps even fighting over the girl's tender flesh. I groan and move closer to my brother's body. No buzzard, I tell myself, will ravage him while I have any strength left.

I dip into my recollection. I know that after the gunfire died out, the ghastly work done, I had teetered on the brink of death, but on the whim of our assailants, I had not been dispatched. My blindness was like a shield that pricked the unpredictable consciousnesses of these killers. Rape and kill a woman is maybe all right, but killing a *blind* man was too much, even for their black hearts. With my helpless brother murdered so callously, the perpetrators walked off, joining their fellows, the hushed laughter of the whole crowd edged with uneasiness at what they had done. If the fool driver and his shotgun guard had not opened up, nobody need have died. But at least they had not killed a blind man. Let God know that!

All the others are dead! The words pound in my head. The killers have not lingered. They scarcely had time to ransack the coach, if that was what they were about. Within minutes, sound of their activity had died out, their voices and scurrying progress sucked away into the immensity of wilderness. No doubt their horses were tethered close by. And what had they achieved besides bloody murder?

But that is hours ago, and now I struggle to cobble my mangled senses. I am alive, that is undeniable, but is my life worth anything? Is it something that I must endure until starvation, heat-stroke or some other evil fate carries me off to join my brother? Will my flesh, within a few hours of my passing, be working its way through a gizzard, my very being re-emerging in the fierce greedy eyes and unimaginable con-sciousness of a turkey vulture? What hope is there for First Lieutenant Raoul Webster, United States Cavalry, third in his graduation class at West Point Academy, now that he is marooned here in the Arizona wilderness among his dead companions, trapped with his grief and anger behind eyes that offer him only blackness?

I press my hands upon the earth, force myself into a sitting position. My limbs feel leaden. I can hear the stream. It gurgles gleefully over the rocks, totally indifferent to the horror that has occurred on its banks. Gingerly, on hands and knees, I feel my way to the water. I dip my hands and wrists into it, welcoming the coolness, then I raise my palms to my face, splash my cheeks, eyes, neck, brow. I rub it into my hair. Where has my hat gone, I wonder. Finally, I cup water to my parched mouth, suck it in. It has a strange bitter taste, but I am not deterred until it occurs to me that I may be supping my own brother's blood. Could it have flowed from his poor, gunshot body down the bank into the stream? Anguish grips me. I cry out.

I return to where my brother is lying. I touch him. He is immensely cold. For a moment I wallow in grief. I make no effort to stem my hot tears. My mind is filled with recollections of him, his laugh, his adventurous spirit, his ambitions, his love for both me and our widowed father. I pray to God that he will be welcomed into Heaven with the blessing he deserves, that he fulfils there the dreams he cherished during his short life.

Then I remember that James has given his life so that I could survive. Were I now to surrender all hope, relinquish all will to live, I would be scorning his sacrifice. I force myself to consider my position. I am alone in a hostile wilderness, hopelessly lost, more helpless than a blind worm. And yet one spark of hope comes to me. Soon, the failure of the coach to arrive at the next way station will be noted. A search party will be sent to find it. If I stay where I am, there is a chance I will be found. I am tempted to pray for my salvation, but pride prevents me. Long ago I vowed that I would pray for others, but never myself. I considered that God would know me well enough to understand my needs.

I sleep and presently awake.

I sense that darkness has come. I can hear bats flickering through the air, making tiny clicking noises. Blind as they may be, they possess uncanny power to navigate. Why can't I be so blessed? I can no longer hear the buzzards, nor even the flies, disputing their pickings. They must all be bloated. From far off, an owl hoots, and suddenly I share the fear felt by rabbit, mouse, squirrel and gopher. There is no mercy, no compassion, in nature. Fear in his prey, is the greatest ally of the predator. Yet it is said that if things are natural, they must be right. I cast these thoughts aside. I draw my coat more tightly about me and lay motionless, feeling the pulse of the ground beneath me. All I can do is wait — wait for rescue or for death.

★ ★ ★

The ratchet-like cry of a squirrel awakes me. I shiver. I can hear birds calling — whippoorwills, night jars. Tiny feet scurry on my hand. As I jerk my hand, a creature clings on. I am aware that it has squirted some fluid onto my skin. With my free hand, I touch a row of pointed scales. I am sure it is a horny toad, the species that squirts blood from its eyelids. I rid myself of its unwanted company.

A sickly sweetness pervades the air

and I remember the proximity of the dead bodies. The sight must be grim after the work of the scavengers. I ache all over, but I force movement into my limbs. I reach across, feel strange reassurance in the closeness of James. He has gone incredibly stiff. As I scramble up, the early warmth of the sun finds me and I realize it is past dawn. I wonder if the search party has already set out to find the coach. Perhaps they have ridden through the night. Perhaps they will arrive at any moment. I must prepare myself.

I empty my bladder, then grope my way to the stream. I stumble over a rock, but retain my footing. I have not eaten for many hours, but I feel no hunger, only nausea. I am refreshing my face in the stream when fear tickles the bumps of my spine. Instinct warns me that I am not alone. I straighten up, straining my ears for errant sound.

'Who is there?' I ask.

The response comes in the familiar

form of a gun being cocked, and then . . . nothing.

'Who is there?' I repeat. 'I cannot see.'

Suddenly a rough hand claws on to my shoulder, grips my coat, spins me around, and the scent of unwashed, rancid body assails my senses. I hear the splash of steps. Somebody else is wading through the stream. Then their voices come, harsh grunting voices that speak in Spanish. There are two of them.

'He cannot see. His eyes are no good.'

'Like Old Santo, eh?'

They laugh, and realization strikes me, brings a constricting sensation to my guts. *They are Apaches.*

'His coat is good. I would like it.'

'What do we do with him. Kill him?'

'No. We will take him to Gokliya. He will decide.'

I am prodded with a gun. I stumble forward, but become disorientated, would fall, but a strong arm threads

24

through mine, guides me with an impatient helpfulness. We move over the rugged ground, one man walking ahead, the other leading me. Desperation rises in me. I am being forced to leave James, but as I pause, I am cuffed across my face and the pain cuts my breath and I can do nothing but stumble on. Sometimes my companion's hard-boned body brushes against me and I realize he is wearing a heavy cartridge belt across his shoulder. There is a wariness in them, as if they themselves are hunted. I try to maintain their pace, for I fear if I delay them they will have little compunction in killing me. And above, the sun rises on its merciless orbit.

It comes to me now. The name they have mentioned — Gokliya. Obviously their leader. I know that white people have another name for him. It is Geronimo.

3

At West Point, we were made fully aware of the Indian troubles. Our instructor, the major with the drooping George Armstrong Custer moustache, told us how he had fought in the campaign against Cochise, how one day his patrol had discovered a prisoner pegged out on the ground, with green rawhide tying his wrists and ankles. The cords had shrunk, constricting to cut off the man's blood flow. His hands and feet had swelled like balloons, but it was his face that was the worst, for it had been broiled red by the sun. The eyelids had been excised, and the eyes were like hard-boiled eggs swimming in a jellied carnage of flesh. He died at the very moment of his rescue.

Gokliya assumed leadership after Cochise's death. His reputation for barbarity is even worse than that of his predecessor. He and his band of renegade Chiricahua Apaches have long been operating deep in Sonora, Mexico. They are the last Apaches to defy white colonization. For some years Gokliya's hatred towards Mexicans has meant that his murderous depredations have been concentrated south of the border, thus leaving Arizona Territory free of Indian trouble. But stories of his deviltry, of his hatred for the White-Eyes, have spread far and wide, and the prospect of Gokliya 'coming north' has always caused hysteria amongst settlers and prospectors. Now, unless my ears deceive me, such fears have become a reality, and my own prospects offer little hope.

I have no option but to comply with the prodding of my captors, and place one foot before the other. Presently, a rope halter is placed around my neck and I am led like a dog. The ground is uneven and punishing and we travel at what seems a relentless pace. No provision is made for the ferocious heat, which soon burns down with the intensity of acid. I wish I had not lost my hat. Flies pester us as we walk. Stops are made all too rarely to sup water from the animal bladder they are carrying. The water is salty and sulphurous. They allow me but a few sips before it is snatched away. Throughout this awesome journey, I am convinced that if I in any way complain or do not respond to their direction, I will be clubbed down or shot. The novelty to them of my blindness will offer no protection. As it is, I am sure they are growing impatient with my clumsy blundering.

I lose all sense of time. The hours of torturous progress seem endless. My captors make no attempt at conversation. At last night brings relieving coolness, coming suddenly like death, and I am allowed to slump to the ground. I am exhausted, but I sleep only fitfully. Insects whine about me. They rouse me constantly and I wave my hands fruitlessly about my head. I am kicked awake before dawn, given a scrap of something akin to cactus to chew on and a sip of water, before the journey is resumed. I realize that I am beyond help from any party seeking the fate of the coach.

As far as I can tell, we walk for three days, but I cannot be certain. I try to banish all thoughts from my mind, concentrate on placing each foot ahead of the other. Apart from the behaviour of my companions, the temperature is the only real delineation between night and day in my world of darkness. Only later will I discover that we have crossed the border into Mexico, that we have entered the *Canon de los Embudos*.

At last, be it the third or fourth day of travel, I am aware that we are descending and our pace is slackening and I hear other Apache voices raised in greeting and surprise, all mingling with the excited yapping of dogs. It is like intruding into an ants' nest. I conclude that we have reached some sort of main camp or rancheria. We halt and I stand for a moment, left unguided, and I feel the eyes of numerous people examining me. The burn of their staring is as tangible as the sun's heat.

'What is he?' somebody asks derisively.

'He is a White-Eye whose eyes have gone black. He is as blind as Old Santo!'

The remark brings a roar of mirth and chatter, and I realize that I am standing within a circle of onlookers, men, women and children.

'His coat is good.'

'You cannot have it. It is mine.'

'Shall we tie him head down over a fire, watch his brains fry?'

'No. It would be better to smear him with honey and bury him in an ant hill! Or burn his feet off.'

'Gokliya will decide.'

'Where is Gokliya?'

'Out hunting.'

'He will decide what we do with him. Now let us put him in a wickiup and guard him. He will not get far if he tries to run away.'

Again the crackle of mirth, and my arms are gripped and I am hustled forward and made to crouch as I am pushed into one of their shelters, a wickiup. It smells of grass and sun-warmed branches. I feel I am in an upturned bird's nest. The air is stifling, but at least I am in shade and glad enough to fall face down onto the ground. The sound of the voices recedes and I believe I am alone. I withdraw into myself, pleased enough for respite. What will happen to me when Gokliya returns? What possible inclination could he have other than to condemn me to some hideous death? The thought concerns me, but I push it from my mind. Overriding all else is the knowledge that my dear brother is dead. It weighs upon me, ever present, crushing me so that my breathing comes in sobs. What will such news do to my father whose heart is already ailing? Anger boils inside me, anger against those who plunged us into this purgatory. And frustration at my own feebleness, always at the mercy of others, unable to stand up for either myself or those I love. Why did the Mexicans waylay the coach? Was there some precious cargo aboard, gold or pay-roll, of which we had no knowledge?

I do not want to die. I will strive for life until the very end, but it would be so much easier if I could see like other men. I know that I am not entirely innocent. I have lusted and sinned as much as anybody else, but nowhere near badly enough to be punished with such affliction. I curse myself. Self-pity will achieve nothing.

I try to calm my mind, try to draw into me the strength of the ground I am sprawled upon, its permanence. It is like a salve to my weariness. I listen to the buzz of flies. I ignore their crawl. At last I sleep.

Something cool and moist awakes me. I wave my hand, brush it away and realize a dog has been licking my face. I roll onto my back, push myself into a sitting position. I hear a laugh, soft and feminine, and a girl's voice comes, but she speaks not in Spanish but in Apache which I cannot understand. There is no harshness in her words. She is young. I smell the closeness of her body, the fragrance of sage and other womanly scents that remind me of other times.

Gently, her hand closes over mine and lifts it to a bowl she is holding. She guides it to my lips. I do not ask myself what I am eating, it is stringy and chewy, perhaps celery of some sort, or cactus, moistened with some animal juices, but suddenly I realize how ravenous I have become. I use my fingers to scoop it into my mouth and she passes me some bread and I wipe the bowl clean. I whisper, '*Grazias*,' and do not know if she understands. She presses a small olla of water into my hands, and I drink, then her voice comes again. She speaks but one word: 'Santo.' And I am conscious that she has been joined by another person. I hear the wheeze of his breathing and know that it is a man, an old man, whose bones click as he lowers himself down beside me and whose body smells of antiquity and smoke.

'Santo,' the girl repeats, and I recall words that I have heard before: *he's as blind as old Santo!*

'Who are you, White-Eye?' His voice creaks with age but shows no hostility, and he speaks good English.

I find my own tongue. 'Raoul Webster. The Mexican bandits let me live when they attacked the stagecoach. They killed my brother.'

Old Santo grunts his understanding. 'I know of the bandits.'

In my mental dimness, I do not pursue his revelation. Instead, I say, 'I would ask that you return me to my people.'

He clears his throat. 'Gokliya will decide. Your eyes . . . how long have you been without them?'

'One year,' I say. 'I was in an accident.' I do not tell him that it was a military accident and that I am in the Army.

After a while, he says, 'I have been blind for many summers. It is not good, but it is not so bad as being dead. There are other senses that we can use. All other senses become sharp. But they can only be used by having the right balance of fear and courage. Fear heightens the senses but it must be controlled by courage. The fear of a coward is quite different from the fear of a warrior.'

'Why does Gokliya hate the white man so?' I ask.

He pauses before answering and there is an edge of anger in his voice. 'Because they steal Apache land. But he hates the Mexicans worst of all, because they killed his wife, children and mother.'

'Why does he come north of the border, then?' I murmur.

'Because the Mexican government offers money for Apache scalps. Two hundred pesos for Apache man, one hundred for Apache woman, fifty for child. Many bounty hunters seek Apache scalps. Gokliya comes north to protect his women and children. His women and children are tired of fighting, of always moving to escape the soldiers and the bounty hunters. Some of the People wish to go to the reservation.'

After a moment I ask, 'Will I be killed?'

'We cannot see inside Gokliya's mind,' Old Santo murmurs. 'He has power and wisdom that no other man has. If he says you die, so be it. Die brave, or it will be worse for you.'

I allow his words to sink in. Eventually I turn my mind to the present.

'The girl who is so good to me. What is her name?'

'Becca,' he says, and then he adds, 'She has a man.'

I am puzzled by his last comment. It is like a warning. It is as if I am a suitor for the girl. This seems absurd.

I am conscious that it is cooler. The

afternoon is reaching towards its brief evening. Old Santo has left me, but I am sure the girl Becca remains, and I think another woman, sitting silently by the entrance to this wickiup. My mind drifts between the comfort their presence somehow brings and the imagined coldness of death. I wonder when Gokliya will return, and when he does how long it will be before my fate is determined.

I sleep.

4

I am dreaming. In my mind's eye, his shadow completely covers me. I feel the heat of his body, along with the ever-present body smells that are Apache. Gokliya has returned from his hunting. Gokliya, meaning he who yawns, whom the Mexicans renamed Geronimo, possessor of strange power. He who should be far to the south in the vastness of Mexico heartland, but, instead, his awesome presence now impinges into my own world. He whose nature has been incited to a homicidal pitch, aimed against Mexicans and White-Eyes alike, by the slaying of his family and the white encroachment into land he considers his. In the image locked into my brain, his eyes possess the craftiness of a buzzard's eyes, and the inhumanity. He is a killing machine. Looming over me, he pauses only briefly. He grunts his contempt, dismissing my existence as worthless scum with a wave of his leathery hand.

'Kill him!'

I awake with a shout. The girl holds a gourd to my mouth and I gulp water down so vigorously that I gag. I calm myself, concentrating on breathing. I tell myself it was only a dream. I wonder if the torment I have experienced has left me delirious, a prisoner not only in my own dark world, but also in the hands of those who would send me along a hideous path of torment to a slow death. I remember Old Santo's words: *Die brave, or it will be worse for you.*

I have experienced only a dream, yet somehow I know that Gokliya has returned.

Presently the girl helps me to my feet, leads me from the wickiup. I conclude it is morning. I can smell camp-fire smoke, hear the cries of children, the bark of a dog, the clink of cooking pots. Fear invades my every sense. Am I about to face my torment? But not immediately. The girl leads me off some way and then we stop. I feel her hands grappling with my belt, and she repeats an Apache word over and over, then she speaks the first English word I have heard her speak:

'Shit!'

The message is clear, but the air is not. It is tainted with the stench of excrement. I squat down and relieve myself, stronger emotions masking any embarrassment I may feel.

As we return to the wickiup, the sounds of camp life seem unconnected with my presence. I feel I am being ignored, but not by my faithful shadow, the girl. I wonder why she is so kind to me. I ask her in Spanish, but she does not understand. Presently she brings me food. I am surprisingly hungry. I believe it is rabbit, or maybe dog. I wonder if I am being afforded a final meal, like a condemned man before being led to the gallows, but decide that Apache pragmatism would not allow that. I conclude that for some reason or other, I have been given a sort of reprieve.

The hours stretch away, turn into days. My existence follows the same pattern. The girl, with whom I have little communication beyond touch, remains my companion, my carer, my turnkey in a prison that has no bars apart from those that prevent my eyes from seeing. The girl shows me patience and consideration, yet I remind myself that she is a 'wild' Indian. Her nature and identity seem incongruous.

Old Santo sometimes returns. I do believe he enjoys talking to me. Sometimes he chants a quiet song. I find his simple colloquy with the spirits soothing. I am ignorant of Indian ritual and the pantheistic spirits of the Apaches, but I learn much from Old Santos's dignified attitude towards his deities.

'Yusn is in every place,' he tells me. 'He cannot be put in one place. He is in every tree, every blade of grass. He is in rain and thunder and sunshine. He would not wish to be kept in one place, like the White-Eye's church.'

He pauses, as if considering whether I am worthy of the story he has to tell. He goes on. 'It is said that White Painted Lady lay down in a storm and that lightning struck her and this caused the birth of Child of Water. Lightning was the child's father and he tested him many times. Child of Water grew into a man and killed a giant who was tormenting the People. He killed him by shooting an arrow into his heel, which was the only unprotected part of his body.'

He also tells me of a great flood.

I draw an assurance from his words. From other stories he tells me, I find an uncanny resemblance to Christian beliefs.

★　★　★

At night there is always another woman in the wickiup. I hear Becca talking to her. I am not ill-treated and am tortured only by the troublesome flies and the recollections and prospects that drift through my mind. I wonder if my brother's body and those of the others have been found and conveyed to more sacred ground. I wonder if my father is aware of the tragedy, what his reaction has been. I speculate as to why my captors are keeping me alive, and cannot find a reason. What possible value can another hungry mouth be to them?

Days and long nights come and go. I listen to voices sounding from outside my bird's nest, but can comprehend little beyond the normal chatter one would associate with a camp of 'wild' Indians. I am growing tired of being ignored. I feel almost affronted. Am I not even worthy of killing? And then one morning, Old Santo again visits me. He says, 'Nantan Lupin is coming.'

His words mean nothing to me.

I shake my head in puzzlement and ask, 'Why has Gokliya not killed me?'

'Because Nantan Lupin is coming to

talk,' he replies impatiently.

'Who is Nantan Lupin?'

'Chief of White-Eye soldiers,' he explains. 'He will talk with Gokliya.'

My heart gives a little skip. I can scarcely believe my ears. In my book, the chief of the White-Eye soldiers is General George Crook, Commander of the Department of Arizona, an officer whom I have never met, though my father has often spoken of him. I know of his reputation as an experienced campaigner who has worked tirelessly to bring about peace in the far West.

'General Crook?' I enquire.

'Yes, the Gray Wolf,' Old Santo replies, and then he asks, 'You know him?'

'Only by name,' I say, anxious not to reveal my army connections.

I am amazed at what I have heard. 'Why should he come here?' I ask.

'He comes to talk with Gokliya about making a treaty. Gokliya will see what he has to offer, but I doubt he will agree it. The White-Eye cannot be trusted.'

'When will he come?' I ask.

'After two suns.'

Old Santo says no more, and as I wrestle with my thoughts and hopes, he leaves.

That night I ponder deeply on what I have been told, and gradually a possible reason for the fact that I am still alive occurs to me. Could it be that I have not been killed because Gokliya intends to use me as a sweetener for General Crook, a bargaining chip to get concessions?

A feeling of euphoria overwhelms me. I believe that God has remembered me. I start thinking of the future and what I must do. After successful treatment to restore my sight, there will be scores to settle. Whoever killed my brother and the other travellers, must be tracked down and brought to justice. That must be my aim.

But I put a lariat around my soaring hopes and drag them back to earth. I remind myself how, in California thirteen years ago, another general,

E.R.S. Canby, went unarmed to talk peace with Indian renegades, and had been murdered in cold blood for his pains. I suspect that Gokliya is equally treacherous. Some military men are so high and mighty that they imagine they are invincible. Is Crook to suffer a similar fate to that of Canby?

* * *

History books will explain far more vividly than any blind man the events of the days that follow. Furthermore, it is not the purpose of this narrative to recount the exact details of General Crook's negotiations with the hostiles, nor in fact do I have the knowledge to undertake such a task. Suffice to say that during the last two days, I have sensed a great agitation amongst the Indians, an undercurrent of fear.

Crook is camped nearby, having come, as he has promised, with only a small party of interpreters. He must be a man of great courage, coming to talk with Indians who are as deadly as so many rattlesnakes and whose observance of any truce is so tenuous. In all, the general meets with Gokliya three times, on each occasion demanding the surrender of the Apaches, conceding only that the Apaches will not be hanged but will be punished with imprisonment in Florida. Gokliya demurs, attempting to justify his barbaric campaign.

At the last conference, when, to my surprise, I am forced to sit behind the chief, I wonder if my presence will be in any way acknowledged by the general, but I hear nothing to that effect. I begin to feel that I am invisible.

Gokliya rambles on. 'There are very few of my men left now. They have done some bad things but I want these bad things rubbed out and let us never speak of them again.'

Later, I will be told how Crook hears the Apache out, his face intransigent, and how eventually Gokliya lapses into Apache rhetoric.

There is one God looking down on

us all. We are all children of one God. God is listening to me. The sun, the darkness, the winds, are all listening to what we now say.

Crook's response is blunt. 'Do not play games with me, Gokliya. I do not need a lecture in religion. Answer me straight, will you surrender or not?'

Gokliya asks for an hour to think.

During this time, I am aware of movement amongst the Apaches, a general shuffling around. A nervous voice shouts instructions, there is a metallic clink as equipment is set up. The truth dawns on me. We are about to have a group photograph taken. It seems totally incongruous, yet it is happening. All I can say is that in the future, if you get the chance to view these pictures, look at the man seated behind Gokliya. Perhaps his appearance is so dishevelled that you will not recognize him as a white man, but he is wearing a fine, though tattered, coat, and his head is lowered as if he is not interested in proceedings. This is far from fact. It is an indication that his eyes see nothing and that his ears are cocked for any clue that he can gain regarding his fate.

He is not kept waiting for long. As several pictures are taken, the camera emits its customary 'pop', causing a ripple of dismay amongst the Indians. At last, with his job completed, the photographer dismantles his equipment and Gokliya's voice comes clearly as he addresses Crook.

'Once I moved about like the wind. Now I give myself up to you. To prove to you that not everything I do is bad, I hand over to you the White-Eye I have looked after, the White-Eye who cannot see. I have not harmed him. Now, do with me what you please. I surrender.'

6

It is four weeks after my release from the Apaches. Professor Otto Rattner has kindly granted me lodging at his fine house in San Francisco while he prepares to treat me. He will not give me any firm assurance that I will regain my sight, but I remain hopeful. He has told me that my brother's body has been taken to Fort Cavendish and buried in consecrated ground. In due course I hope to discuss matters with my father and we shall decide where James's final resting place will be.

I frequently scratch my head. Its itch drives me crazy. Professor Rattner tells me that I have head-lice, caught from my time with the Apache. He has had my hair cut off, so that I am almost bald. What little hair I have, I must wash twice each day. He has given me some medication to rub into my scalp, oil of sassafras, and I have to wear a cotton cap which no doubt makes me look idiotic. At least I am spared sight of my own reflection in a mirror. So far the treatment has not provided a cure. I hope his treatment of my eyes is more successful than his medication.

As I wait impatiently for Professor Rattner to start work on my lack of vision, I realize he is a busy and successful practitioner. I hear the footsteps of many other patients in the corridor beneath my room. Often their words of satisfaction are audible to me.

One day, I receive a visitor. He is a Louisiana man, a banker called Edwin Carleton, and he tells me that he is the father of the young lady who was aboard the coach on the horrific day of the hold-up. Despite the time that has since elapsed, he is obviously still in a high state of agitation. I sense this as he passes me a slender cheroot and helps me light it. From the heaviness of his breathing, I gain the impression that he is a fairly large man.

He asks me to relate my recollection of events, and I tell him how I was found by the Apaches, taken to Gokliya's camp and subsequently passed over to General Crook. Thereafter, how the good general placed me in the hands of a young subaltern who was as full of ambition as I once was. He conducted me, by rail, to San Francisco and to the home of Professor Rattner.

Edwin Carleton accepts my story without comment but makes a surprising revelation. 'When the search party discovered the coach, there were two bodies missing. One was obviously yours, and the other was my daughter Gabriella. Her uncle, my brother, had been shot through the head, but there was no trace whatsoever of her. I do not know if Gabriella is alive or dead. I can only assume that she was abducted, but the only reason for this I can imagine would be to demand a ransom. It is well known that I am not a poor man.'

'But no demand for money has been made?' I enquire.

'No, Lieutenant Webster, nothing. If she still survives, I am sure she will have been taken to Mexico. But it's a big country down there and we have no clue as to who her kidnappers are or where they are from. That's why I've come to you. In the hope, you understand, that you may be able to remember something, some clue as to the identity of these men.'

'I am equally anxious to trace them,' I say. 'They murdered my brother and I am determined they should be brought to justice.'

'But can you remember anything about them?' he persists.

'Mr Carleton, it is very difficult for a blind man. All I can say is that I am sure they were Mexican.'

'And nothing else?'

I scratch my head.

'You remember nothing else?' Carleton repeats.

'Nothing,' I say, 'apart from . . . '

'What?' His voice is tainted with exasperation.

'When I was with the Apache, a blind Indian called Old Santo said he knew of the bandits.'

'And you asked him to explain?'

I take a breath. I feel ashamed. 'No.'

'Why not!'

'I have posed myself that question a hundred times,' I admit. 'All I can say is that I was too concerned with my own fate at that time. I should have asked him to tell me all he knew, but the fact was I expected to die an unpleasant death at any moment.'

I take a final draw on my cheroot, feel for my ash-tray and stub it out.

I hear Carleton breathing heavily, and then steady himself as he gets his emotions under control. Eventually he says: 'I understand, Lieutenant Webster. As you said, it is not easy for a blind man. But what you have told me is the first glimmer of a clue we have had.'

'Perhaps,' I say, scarcely able to hold back my excitement, 'I can talk with Old Santo again. Perhaps he will know where we can find the murderers.'

It is apparent that he does not share my excitement. 'You have not been told what was in today's *San Francisco Chronicle*?'

'No,' I say.

'There's a story about Gokliya, and how he's gone back on his word to Crook. He's broken out from the reservation at San Carlos, apparently heard word some white folks planned to string him up. His Chiricahuas have gone 'wild' again. The Army went after them, but couldn't catch them. They're probably deep in the Sonora Mountains by now. That's a vast stretch of territory. Trying to find them will be like hunting a needle in a haystack, Lieutenant Webster.'

I bury my face in my hands, cursing myself for not pressing Old Santo when I had the chance. I think of my dark days in that wickiup, of the girl, of the old blind man. If only I can communicate with them again! A thought comes to me.

'After Professor Rattner's treatment,'

I say, 'when I've got my sight back, I'll find those Apaches.'

'You'll need a few weeks to recover, a few weeks before you're fit enough to go hunting for wild Indians.'

'Once I can see again,' I say, 'my aim will be to find the men who killed my brother, to bring them to justice. At the same time, I will do my utmost to discover your daughter's fate.'

In that moment another thought plagues me. I wonder if Carleton is being naïve about what has happened to Gabriella, if he has overlooked the fact that men will sometimes kidnap a female person for reasons other than those motivated by money. Particularly in the case of a girl as pretty as I am certain Gabriella is. But I say nothing of this.

'If you bring her back to me, I'll pay you a reward bigger than anything you ever dreamed of.'

'I only want one reward, Mr Carleton, and that's the restoration of my sight.'

I feel his hand grasp mine. We shake and he says, 'We must pray that God will give us the rewards we so earnestly desire.'

★ ★ ★

It is three days since the visit of Edwin Carleton. Our conversation has stirred up all sorts of wild dreams in me. Dreams to avenge my brother's death, though as yet I have not hit upon a positive plan.

I do believe Professor Rattner's treatment of the oil of sassafras is working. My scalp has ceased to itch. In view of what lies ahead, I feel this is a good omen. No doubt the treatment will prove an ordeal, and the expectation involved, but one I will gladly suffer. I wish a guarantee of success would come with it, but no matter how hard I press the professor, he will promise nothing. All he will say is that he has treated three other persons and restored their sight.

I ask myself: when your sight returns, what will you most wish to see? And the answer is always the same. James's grave at Fort Cavendish. I have this strange feeling that I will be able to communicate with him, to explain how sorry I am at what happened — and how I will do my utmost to bring his murderer to justice.

The weeks slip by. I become confident in moving around my room, my touch always finding its objective. It is as if my fingertips possess vision. I can also sense the closeness of solid objects by a change in the air as it touches my face. Professor Rattner is so surprised by my adeptness, that he believes my sight is returning and that the passage of time is having a commodious effect. He suggests I wear a blindfold. But sadly this brings no change to my abilities. I am equally proficient, with or without the blindfold.

Now, at last, the professor commences his treatment. He works tirelessly. To me, his methods seem revolutionary, not at all as I expected. He massages my scalp, neck and the knuckles of my spine with strong, probing fingers, and applies strong-smelling, aromatic oils. He claims he is moving the fluids of the body, blood, lymph, black and yellow bile, moving them in the correct polar directions.

He makes me exercise the movement of my eyeballs extensively, rolling them up and down, back and forth till they ache. I feel he is trying to make me see inside my skull. Then he applies warm compresses and has me resting back, perfectly still. He directs light into my eyes, so he says, but I see not a glimmer and my eyes have grown incredibly sore.

He constantly urges me to show patience, and I do my utmost. I feel like an escapologist striving to burst free from a huge black sack, but for me the sack is made of thick rubber which becomes increasingly elastic as I struggle in vain to break it open.

Gradually the sense of failure seeps

deeper and deeper into my soul, though I try not to show it. Rattner appears to spend longer studying his books and notes. Sometimes I hear him murmuring softly to himself as he studies. I suspect he is trying to find out why his treatment brings not the slightest success, why I should be so different from the others he has cured.

Eventually, not even he can conceal his disappointment and frustration. One day he admits, 'Raoul, my attempts to alleviate your symptoms have failed. There is nothing else I can try. I felt convinced the blindness was an impediment of the spirit rather than of the body, but I was wrong. I believe both corneas to be scarred beyond redemption, at least with medical knowledge at its present level.'

I believe I weep at this moment.

Rattner tries to console me. 'Some people claim,' he says, 'that sight is a curse, that we are better off without it.'

I find this hard to believe.

If only there were a glimpse of light,

just a pinprick, which I could reach for, but there is nothing save eternal, claustrophobic nothingness. I am devastated, more so even than when realization of my blindness first struck me. Then, I was convinced that the disablement would be of a temporary nature. Now my spirits have plunged and I languish in the deepest depression, blaming my affliction on a Godly whim. I close my eyes, burying myself in a double obscurity. I wish my eyes had been burned out with a hot iron. Then I would not have cherished this futile hope for so long.

Professor Rattner tries to cheer me, but I know that he, like me, is greatly discouraged. I am uncertain of my future. Obviously there is no place for a blind man in military service. My days in uniform are long finished. Rattner has told me not to abandon all hope of regaining my sight, but I am not convinced. He has also mentioned that there are simple employments that a handicapped person can undertake and different skills that can be learned, but again I am not convinced. And at night my nightmares grow more profound. My mind's eye seems sharper and more vivid than ever my true vision was. Over and over, I see my brother, and hear him calling to me for help, *Raoul, Raoul*, and I remain motionless, unable to respond to his pleas, and his words linger to haunt me . . . *Don't harm him. He is blind!*

And then the blast of the gun.

Professor Rattner does not press me to move on, but I feel that ultimately I shall have to return to the East. My mood is not helped by news that my father is ill. James's death has, by all accounts, left him a broken man.

But today I am surprised by a further visit from Edwin Carleton. I imagined that he would have little time or use for me now that I was condemned to continuing blindness. He has a cold manner, but none the less he expresses consolation regarding the failure of the treatment. He tells me that he has still heard nothing of his daughter's fate.

'Webster,' he says in his slow Louisiana way, 'I have been talking to a former detective, Jonas Simpson. He has also worked at an Indian agency. He knows the ways of Indians. I have offered him a substantial reward if he gets information about Gabriella. But he is convinced that the only means by which this can be achieved is by contacting the Apaches, a task he considers too dangerous for himself. He does not know this old man Santo you mentioned, nor does he trust Gokliya. He says that the only means we can get information from the Apaches is for you to go, because they befriended you previously.'

'Me!' I gasp. 'What hope would a blind man have of finding them? The Army's been trying to find them for weeks without success.'

He offers me a cigar, but I decline, feeling too depressed to enjoy the pleasure of tobacco. I hear his match strike and then the suck of his lips as he lights up.

'It would *not* be a matter of you finding them,' he says. 'It would be a matter of them finding you.'

His words astound me. The reality hits me. 'You mean I would be human bait?'

'Not exactly,' he says. 'They have treated you kindly before. I have no doubt they will do the same again. This time you must get Old Santo to reveal the identity and location of the Mexican bandits. It is the only way, Webster. The only way to find your brother's killers . . . and the whereabouts of my daughter.'

I spend a minute allowing his words to sink in. Momentarily, my original reaction that the suggestion is outrageous recedes.

Eventually I say, 'I would need somebody to guide me. Gokliya is still south of the border, by all accounts, probably in the Sonora Mountains. The country is vast. I need somebody who knows that country.'

'Jonas Simpson is such a man,' he says. 'He is not keen, but I will offer him a financial reward he cannot resist.'

The prospect of what he is suggesting has my heart beating faster. My initial doubts come flooding back. I remind myself that Gokliya has never shown me friendship. I was simply a tool he found useful at the time. Otherwise there was little doubt that I would have ended up as a mutilated corpse.

'I cannot see how such a venture can succeed,' I say, speaking my thoughts aloud.

'Webster, there is nobody else who can get anywhere near the Apaches. You are the only chance.' He pauses. The aroma of his cigar is rich in my nostrils. Maybe I will have one after all.

'Will you do it?' he says

His question hangs in the air, as if it is on quivering wings. I swallow, feel the muscles in my jaw taking control. The words slide from my lips, suddenly possessing a will of their own.

'Yes. I will do it.'

He emits a long sigh which I take as indicating relief.

'Webster,' he says, 'in the hope that you would agree to undertake the task, I have already drawn up a plan. After you have found the Apaches and extracted the information that we require, you and Simpson must report back to the town of Maverick Springs. Simpson has arranged for some of his trusted friends, led by a Frenchman called Louis Dupont, to wait there. Maverick Springs is in southern Arizona on the Jiricilla River. Simpson knows where it is.'

'I have heard of it,' I say.

'There will be a party of six men waiting. They will be men familiar with Mexico; Simpson will ensure that. It will be their task to rescue my daughter from wherever she is held.'

'If she is still alive,' I say.

'Yes, yes. I believe she is.'

There are many more matters to be discussed, but right now I do not have the stomach for further talk. I am overawed by what I have agreed to. Carleton is clutching at straws, and I am the longest straw — and the flimsiest. In Carleton's estimation, I know, my survival is of little consequence provided he achieves his aim. I console myself with the thought that if the mission proves successful, I will be closer to the man who so callously murdered my brother, closer to somehow inflicting upon him the fate he deserves.

7

It is three weeks later. I had thought of Jonas Simpson as a brave man, but now I am doubtful as to the extent to which he can be trusted, for he is constantly cursing his luck. He often mentions the possible disasters that I strive to put from my mind. He is obviously a man who is well versed in both the terrain and the ways of the Indians, and I am wondering if this very knowledge is what makes him so fearful of the future. Admittedly, trekking into this vast, wild country, seeking hostile Indians, your only hope of avoiding the most hideous fate resting in the fact that a blind man, whom once the Apaches spared, is your companion, offers little to enthuse over. But Simpson is greedy and he has been paid well by Edwin Carleton, and if our mission is successful, there will no doubt be further financial reward forthcoming.

I mentioned that we are 'seeking' the Indians. This is incorrect of course. The Army has been seeking them for weeks, crossing the border to do so under a special agreement with the Mexican government. So have the local *rurales*, not to mention swarms of bounty hunters anxious to make money out of Apache scalps. But none has established contact. The chances of the nervous Simpson and his blind associate might seem hopeless — unless one important fact is considered. We are not seeking Gokliya's band. We are merely placing ourselves in a position whereby *they can find us*. Hopefully they will recognize me, and my presence will prick their interest, their inquisitiveness, and prevent out immediate slaughter.

My main task, as I ride, is to hold aloft a white flag, tied to a length of cane. But such a sign of truce does not mean that I am unarmed. Before leaving San Francisco, I purchased a small Derringer pistol, four inches long, of large calibre and deadly at close range. I have had a concealed extension made to the pocket of my coat, within the lining, and the gun slots into this most neatly. Thus, nobody will realize that I have a gun, for I am anxious to preserve my appearance of being completely vulnerable. This very vulnerability, strangely, gives me a protective shield and has saved my life more than once. The gun is ready-loaded and even if I am unable to see a target at which to aim, a single shot to my head may well be preferable to an agonizing death at the hands of torturers.

And despite the menace that threatens us, I cannot help but revel in the wonder of the country through which we travel — the freshness of the morning air, the joyous voice of nature, the overwhelming presence of the mountains, the creaking of tree-branches touched by breeze, the limitless skies, the sense of clean and unspoiled vastness. I may be sightless, but my awareness of the great outdoors is no less real.

⋆　⋆　⋆

I suspect that Carleton, as he waits in San Francisco, cares little about my fate, nor about my quest to avenge my brother's murder, but he sees me as the only means of tracing his daughter's abductors, and the fact that our objectives are closely aligned, has created a temporary bond between us, one which, I am sure, will disappear immediately he no longer has a use for me.

'I reckon we've been watched ever since we crossed at Nogales,' Simpson confides one evening as he prepares supper. 'Old Gokliya's got spies out for sure. They can cut us down any time they choose. This whole crazy venture makes me feel downright jittery.'

I nod. Maybe he is right, but I am resigned to whatever Fate holds in store. I see no evil, hear no evil, apart from my companion's grim expectations and his ungracious behaviour. He grumbles endlessly that he must remain vigilant; even at night he can take only minimal sleep in case we are surprised. This, unfortunately, is true, but there is nothing I can do about it. He tells me that at night the wolves watch us, great pale lobos, their eyes glinting in the firelight. I imagine them loping through the darkness like ghosts, their long noses to the ground.

I have no idea why Edwin Carleton has placed his trust in such a man as Simpson. In my blind state, I need certain assistance and guidance, but this is only forthcoming in the most grudging way. As we travel, we talk but little, for we are not well suited as travelling partners. I suspect that, should the time be ripe, he, like Carleton, will dump me with scarcely a second thought. I am certain the only motive for his undertaking this journey is the financial reward that Edwin

Carleton has promised.

I seek companionship in the depths of my mind. I ask myself what I will do when, and if, I eventually track down those responsible for James's death, but I can come up with no answer. I am reliant on Fate presenting me with some means of achieving my aims.

In this season of the fall, here in the Sonora Mountains, the days remain hot, but the nights are cooler. I know that these mountains lack crests. Instead, there are many flat uplands, thick with saguaros and arid land scrubs.

I revel in my strange detachment from the dangers that Simpson is certain surround us. He blasphemes and frequently tells me not to be so open as I refresh myself in a stream, not to advertise our presence so blatantly. I remind him that it is the very purpose of our mission to reveal our presence to the Apaches. Unless they find us, we are wasting our time.

He reluctantly agrees, but says when

you're in Indian country, it's not natural to go about as if you are on some schoolchild's treat. He tells me that I always close my eyes when I am thinking. He tells me that he wishes they were closed more often, for I seem not to overwork my brain.

He is a good one to talk about advertising our whereabouts, for I am conscious of *his* whereabouts, by his grumbling, and by the fact that he breaks wind like thunder at every opportunity. But I remind myself that without the benefit of his company I will be hopelessly lost and have little chance of fulfilling my aims. My tactile fluency has not yet reached perfection.

In my dark world, days and nights seem to merge and I lose track of time. At nights I dream of James, hear again his last frantic words: *Do not harm him. He is blind.* And the crash of the gun awakes me. My body is bathed with the sweat of anger.

For what reason was his life taken? He had never harmed anybody, yet he has died by cold-blooded murder.

It seems we have been in these mountains a long while. We have passed near two copper mines, many villages, haciendas, adobes, grazing cattle and *vaqueros*, but have not established contact with the locals. Once, we come to an abandoned village where the wind sighs through the walls of empty huts made from the stalks of thorny ocotillo. Simpson, in his usual pessimistic state, swears we would not be welcome. Several times, also, he has reported sighting troops of *rurales* in their crossed bandoleers and kepis. Once, he swore he saw black hair bundles dangling from their belts. These half-wild *soldados* are scouring the country. They, like us, are seeking Apaches, though for different reasons. As they pass, we are glad enough to find seclusion within trees or behind rocks.

Now, from what I can understand, we are moving amid a labyrinth of canyons, all of which contain water, mostly fast running. I listen to the birds, and by their calls I am able to recognize different hours of the day. In the evenings, gnats come to plague us.

There is no lack of game or grass. I must give Simpson his due. He is adept at living off the land. Sometimes he leaves me for hours sitting beside our mesquite fire, until I reach the edge of despair, believing that he has deserted me for good, but so far he has always returned, usually with a wild turkey or rabbit, and once a small hog, for the pot.

Frequently we wend our way through dense pine forests where the air is redolent with balsam and the ground is treacherous and matted with scrub oak. At other times we cross slopes littered with rocks and boulders of all sizes, and we are obliged to deviate. All the while, I hold my white flag aloft. Simpson tells me he sees distant mirrors flashing in the sun.

I have named my sorrel Patience; he is proving a good friend to me. Before we crossed the border, Jonas Simpson bought him for me from a horse-dealer at the cost of ten dollars, plus a double-rigged 'Rimfire' saddle for forty. It was perhaps the best thing Simpson has ever done for me. Patience is, I am told, chestnut in colour with a blaze down one side of his face, and is sure-footed. He seems to understand my affliction, and remains still whilst I saddle him and fit his bridle. He never carries me beneath low branches. His stride is powerful and free, and I never need to use the quirt. I am immensely fond of him. He follows Simpson's horse diligently, his navigation and understanding of the trail so much better than mine. He even responds when I call him, and, most important, senses danger when it is present, blowing through his nostrils and drawing air in noisily. Yet he is not without spirit, and we share little horse jokes that only he and I can understand.

At evening camp, we hobble our animals at some distance and bring them in with the advent of darkness.

They thus get the best grazing in both areas.

One afternoon Simpson finds the evidence of Apache presence. Upon the trail, he tells me, are assorted items plundered from the Mexicans — dresses, saddle, bridles, letters, flour, onions and other items. Apparently, the clothing is heavily stained with blood. No doubt Apaches have struck terror into some settlement, showing no mercy. The discarded foodstuffs are comparatively fresh which indicates that our quarry is not far away. All have been dumped, the Indians, obviously, having more valuable items to carry.

That evening I persuade Simpson to build a small fire on open ground and, once ablaze, to place a blanket over it and suddenly lift it clear so that a column of black smoke rises upwards. Whilst unleashing a constant stream of profanity, cursing himself for complying with my crazy wishes, he repeats the action several times, allowing further smoke-shafts to rise. At least that is what I hope he is doing.

It is my belief that by this means we will arouse the curiosity of the Indians. Previously they may have felt that we were unworthy of their attention. Now, I hope, our audacity will draw them to us.

On taking to my bedroll this night, I am unable to sleep. I listen to what I believe are the shrill yaps of kit foxes, but after a while I wonder if the cries are emanating from human throats, and they suddenly sound more eerie.

Come morning, just after I have risen from my blanket and am doing what I can to help in the preparation of breakfast, we are startled by a sound like rushing water.

'Covey of quail,' Simpson explains uneasily. 'Something's scared 'em for sure.'

Then comes something worse: an awful swishing whisper, like the sound of a hoe digging into flinty earth, followed by a thud and vibration. I realize that an arrow has been fired into a tree trunk scant feet from us. Simpson unleashes a grunted blasphemy and there follows an awesome silence, a moment, I sense, in which we hover between life and death. But I am no stranger to such moments and soon I hear the rustling of foliage. A familiar scent of rancidity wafts to me and I know, without Simpson's hissed 'They found us!' that the Apaches are at last here.

In Spanish I shout out: 'I am Webster, a friend of Gokliya. I am blind! I have come to visit Old Santo!'

There is truculence in the voice that answers. 'We know who you are, White-Eye. We know you are fools to come into Apache country where you will die.'

'I ask that I may speak with Old Santo before I die,' I say, trying to keep the tremor from my words.

Strangely, what I have said arouses a ripple of laughter.

'It is best you die first, then you can speak with Old Santo in the spirit land.

He has already passed over.'

Dismay seeps through me, making my limbs seem leaden. Old Santo's death is something I haven't contemplated. *I have been blind for many summers. Blindness is not good, but it is not as bad as being dead.* I wonder if he has changed his mind now.

'White-Eye,' the voice comes mockingly, 'would you prefer an arrow or a bullet to send you on your way?'

'I would prefer to speak with Gokliya first,' I say. 'He will not insult a blind man who comes to visit him. I understand that he respects courage as he respects the truth.'

I hope I have struck a sensitive cord. Hospitality towards friendly visitors is said to be a quality of Apache culture, yet I know I am stretching this concept to the full.

I await the response. I can hear Simpson murmuring over and over how we are pushing our heads into a noose, how there are at least six of the red devils, all armed to the teeth. As for myself, I am beset by a curious calmness, and with it a hope that, with Old Santo dead, Gokliya has the knowledge we seek — the identity of the Mexican killers. Perhaps he will also know something of the abducted girl Gabriella Carleton,

Almost inevitably, the Apache voice comes again.

'Very well, Webster. We will take you to Gokliya. Perhaps this time, he will roast your brains from your head, like he should have done before!'

'Good,' I say, sensing I was playing some sort of macabre game with our Apache guests. 'Our horses are hobbled in a thicket. We must fetch them.'

'Do not worry,' comes the response. 'We have brought them for you!'

8

'I do not like this,' Simpson whispers into my ear, and there is an edge in his tone, an edge of fear, that I have grown to know. We are being taken to meet Gokliya.

'Why not?' I murmur. 'Surely this is what we wanted all along. My only hope is that Gokliya will be co-operative. After all, he hates Mexicans even more than us.'

'It was my intention to meet your friend Santo, but not in Gokliya's rancheria. It would've been best if we'd met him at some secret place. But now the man's dead and so will we be pretty soon, if I'm not mistaken.'

'Having let us come this far,' I argue, 'I don't think Gokliya will kill us.'

'Webster,' he gasps exasperatedly, 'can't you understand? You are lucky. You are blind. He has nothing to fear from you. But I can see. Can you imagine that once I have seen Gokliya's hideaway, he'll let me ride away and tell all and sundry!'

Why has he not thought of this before? His greed for Carleton's money blinded him to the hazards.

'I was a fool,' he goes on. 'I should never had taken this crazy job on. Not all the money in the world is worth it.'

'One thing the Apaches admire,' I say, 'is courage. Provided we show it at all times, we'll be all right.'

He grunts his doubts, but at the moment he has no option but to comply with whatever our captors have in mind for us. It seems they will do nothing without Gokliya's approval.

We are far closer to the Apache camp than we had imagined. It seems only a short time before we reach it. We ride through a narrow corridor of rock. I sense its constriction as if we are passing through the neck of a bottle. It echoes with the sound of our animals' hoofs. But shortly, the echoic atmosphere has gone and I sense that we are entering the inner sanctum, the hidden place. The air is thickened with the taint of camp-fire smoke. Once again, I sense that Indians are crowding about us, and my horse Patience jumps as a dog snaps at his legs. We trail to a stop and I feel a hand slap my knee and a voice says, 'Dismount!'

Having slipped from my saddle, I am aware that somebody has grasped my reins, a woman, and is taking my sorrel away.

'Look after him well,' I say. 'I will need him when I leave.'

Patience neighs wildly but then grows quiet as he is led off.

Hands are placed on my shoulders and I am forced to sit on the ground. I cross my legs. Simpson is beside me. He always smells, but now it is different. He is sweating with fear.

The babble of conversation around us grows quiet. It is as if we are in the presence of some dignitary. I guess we are.

'I knew you were coming, Webster.

My power has told me.'

I steady my breathing. I remember the voice well, though previously it had never been addressed to me directly.

'You are Gokliya,' I say.

'I am Gokliya.'

I pause, gathering my wits. 'We came to see Old Santo, but I hear he is dead.'

'He died of a tired heart. All my people are tired, tired of being hunted.'

'But Nantan Lupin promised you could live in peace. That is why you gave up.'

I hear him sigh heavily. It is a while before he speaks again.

'I trusted Nantan Lupin. I still trust him. But he does not speak for all the White-Eyes. We learned that they intended to kill us. That is why we ran away. That is why we have come to this land of the scalp hunters again.'

'Nantan Lupin would have protected you,' I say.

'He cannot be everywhere. He does not have eyes in the back of his head.' Again he pauses. 'Why do you come here, Webster? Why do you come, when I can kill you in the time it takes to blink?'

'I come because I am like you,' I say. 'I am saddened by what has happened. Mexicans killed my brother, just like they killed your family. They attacked our stagecoach and killed him. I seek to punish them, but I need to find them first. I need to know who they are and where they are. Old Santo told me he knew of these murderers, but Old Santo is gone now and so I am asking you for help, because I believe that you will know who and where these enemies are.'

'You are a brave man to come here,' Gokliya says. 'That is why I have listened to you.'

'But do you know about the Mexican murderers?'

'Gokliya knows many things. Inside him, he has great power.'

'I understand that. It is why I am here. It is why I trust you with my life.'

'You are crazy,' he says. 'I shall be

sorry to kill you.'

'You will gain nothing by killing us,' I say. 'All I ask is that you tell us what you know about the Mexicans.'

And then he murmurs words that are sweet to my ears.

'The leader of the Mexicans you seek, is called Jesus Escobedo. He has a hacienda near to the village of Santa Janos. His men have taken the scalps of my people. He has made his hacienda into a fortification. It is not easy to attack, otherwise I would have killed him long ago.'

'I am grateful for this knowledge,' I say. 'I believe Gokliya is a wise leader and one day soon he will find the peace he deserves.'

'How can you, a man without eyes, gain revenge against Escobedo?' he asks.

I hesitate for a moment, then I find my words.

'As I say, Gokliya, I am like you. I too have a great power inside me. Now that we know where Escobedo can be found, we shall return across the mighty river where a force of White-Eyes awaits to destroy Escobedo. That will be good for the Apaches.'

'Webster,' he says, and there is mirth in his voice, 'you should be an Apache.'

Escobedo . . . Jesus Escobedo. The name nestles in my mind like a serpent feeding on hatred, but I bridle my thoughts.

'There is something else, Gokliya,' I say. 'The Mexicans abducted a white girl from the stagecoach. Do you know of her?'

He sighs. 'Gokliya knows of many things. But he does not know everything.'

Disappointed, I nod my understanding.

I chance my luck. 'So you will not kill us?'

'Not tonight,' he grunts. 'Not if you do not bring trouble. In two or three days I will decide.'

Simpson has remained silent, leaving the talking to me. I have the feeling that he wishes he could disappear all together. Particularly now we know the identity and location of the bandits.

We are shown hospitality. We are brought food, and when a bowl of stew is given to me I feel a gentle touch on my arm and a girl's voice whispers, 'Webster.' Within the voice is an undercurrent of joy that makes my insides tingle.

'Becca,' I murmur, and suddenly I realize how pleased I am to be with this gentle girl again, she who cared for me so kindly after the Apaches first took me. I place my hand over hers and there is a communication between us, a strange union that is without words, for her knowledge of English and Spanish is as scant as mine is of Apache. I rest my thumb on her pulse, feel how it is racing. She laughs, whispering my name. I suddenly sense that there is a delight in her candescent enough to warm my soul.

To my surprise I hear Gokliya laugh. 'Becca has moped like a lovesick calf since you went away.'

I smile and wonder what I have done to merit such affection from this girl. She is giving me her presence, which is something quite different from anything else I have experienced.

★   ★   ★

The stew is chewy but good. Perhaps it is dog. After we have eaten, Gokliya tells me that we must stay overnight, and tomorrow he will decide what he will do with us. I am a little daunted by his comment, for it reminds me that within this impression of affability, we are his prisoners, and if he wishes to kill us, the option is still his.

Through the rest of the day, Becca seems content enough to sit with me, our hands linked, and I wish we had words to express our feelings but that is not possible. She rests my hand between her breasts.

Close by, I hear Simpson snoring. Presently, when he comes awake he says: 'Webster, I don't want to wait here until they decide to kill me. We have the information we came for. Tonight, I shall get away.'

I grunt with alarm. 'That would be foolish,' I whisper. 'They're sure to catch you and they will be angry.'

'It's a chance I've got to take. It's all right for you. They won't harm you.'

'They won't harm you if you show courage,' I argue. 'They're constantly on the move, anyway. By the time we get back across the border, they'll have moved on. So whatever knowledge you have of this camp will be old news.'

I reach forward, grasp the sleeve of his coat. 'With you gone,' I say, 'I'll never get back across the border.'

He shrugs my hand away. 'That's your problem, Webster.'

I am angry. He is placing everything in jeopardy.

'Don't be a fool!' I snap at him.

He doesn't respond.

Becca smoothes my brow with her fingers. It is the most delightful feeling imaginable. It somehow eases the worry and pain from my head and the nagging wounds from my soul. Frequently, she whispers my name and we laugh together. Her touch moves to my moustache and beard and she laughs. The hair on my face always amuses her, for Indians do not grow beards. Later I rest on my pallet, but James probes into my mind and with him a strange threat of violence and of unfinished work. And quite suddenly, I recall the moment preceding his death . . . the words of his killers. Why had it not occurred to me before? *Jesus! Kill him!*

All along, I'd imagined 'Jesus' to be a taking of Christ's name in vain. Now I viewed it differently, as a demand upon *Jesus* Escobedo, and thus a confirmation of Escobedo's personal guilt of my brother's murder.

As I lapse into sleep, I am cursing him, cursing him with all the bitterness in my soul.

On waking, I sense that it is evening. The air has cooled, the noises of the encampment are hushed. Becca has left me. I call to Simpson, but he does not answer. I hope he hasn't embarked upon his crazy plan. I reach around, discover a cholla of water that the girl has left for me. I drink and feel refreshed.

Shortly, Becca returns. She helps me up, guides me to a wickiup. I rest down upon a buffalo robe. I wish I could communicate with her and find out what she is thinking. We speak to each other, but in different languages. It is deeply frustrating. I wonder where Simpson is. Has he been taken to another wickiup?

But tragedy is beckoning, like the gnarled finger of a witch.

Later I am startled by a cry — an anguished cry. At first, I believe it to be some wild creature in great pain, but then the truth dawns on me. The cry is repeated three times, each time more horrific. I sit up, hear Apache voices from outside.

I call, 'Becca!' and she comes to me

from the far side of the wickiup. Her hands touch me and she makes a soothing sound, but there is a tenseness in her. I know that something bad has happened. Presently the night grows quiet. Becca indicates that I should lie down again which I do, though my body is trembling and frustrated in my inability to discover for myself what has happened.

In the morning Gokliya visits me. His breath reeks with tiswin, the Apache beer. He is angry and this frightens me.

'Your White-Eye friend tried to run away,' he grunts. 'He was a fool. He is dead now — *muerto*!'

I sigh with anguish.

I do not ask how Simpson has died. I know his death will not have been easy, that is enough.

9

Not even Becca can now raise my spirits. I have sunk into the deepest depression. There seems no light in my black world. I sense that Gokliya's friendship towards me has drained away, that it is at present completely beneath his dignity to even think of me. I am of no use to him now. In fact I am of no use to anybody. I seem helpless to do anything to bring relief to this gloom. I can imagine no way that I can get back across the border into the United States. Even on the north side of the border, the terrain is wild and totally inhospitable. Through my own rashness, my own unwillingness to accept the limitations of my disability, I have buried myself in a black pit from which there is no escape. I believe I am weeping, for my cheeks are moist, but I am beyond caring. I might just as well have died alongside Simpson.

But despite everything, I have at least one friend. Becca is the only flicker of compassion, of warmth. She attends to my needs with unflagging concern. No doubt she has learned her caring ways from looking after Old Santo over the years. I wonder if she is his daughter, if she has grieved his loss as I have the loss of my brother. She leads me about the camp on short walks, and on one occasion I cling to her soft body and whisper my gratitude and I do believe she understands. As for the other Indians, no one seems to come near me. Am I to be left indefinitely in this limbo world? But as I ponder on this it dawns on me that I can have no place in a band of hostile Apaches, that circumstances, sooner or later, will mean my position will be resolved, and there is little mercy in the make-up of Gokliya, unless he sees some benefit to himself or his people as the end result.

My head is itching again. I grow frantic with scratching and my supply of oil is long exhausted. Becca leads me to a stream, washes my hair, then rubs wet, slimy mud into my scalp and it no longer itches. Afterwards, she washes it again. I squeeze her hand in gratitude and hear her laugh. It sounds like sunshine. I cannot understand her. I sense that she is vibrant with happiness, and know that for some reason I am the source of this happiness. She cares for me as a mother would care for a child, yet somehow she never makes me feel subordinate.

It seems dreams come to haunt me each time I venture into slumber. Tonight is no exception. I have found Escobedo and am grappling with him, pressing my thumbs into his eyes so that he will be as blind as I am. He is screaming and squirming. His eyes pop out from their sockets, bloodying my thumbs and hands, and I know now that we are fighting on level terms. He is strong, but, as we grapple, I find his windpipe and start to squeeze. As I writhe to one side, I feel the slash of a knife against the side of my ribs, but I ram my knee into his belly, thrust him aside — and in that instant I hear Becca screaming and realize I am no longer asleep. I am gripping a man's wrist. It is greasy, slips in my grasp, and I know suddenly that it is not Escobedo with whom I am struggling, but somebody else. Somehow, I push him back, aware that Becca has joined in the fight, dragging the attacker away from me.

Gradually, I realize that there is a ferocious struggle going on, of which I am no longer part, and suddenly the wickiup seems filled with people and loud voices. I recognize Gokliya's stentorian shout, commanding order.

'Take him away. Take him away. Bind him up!' Then the commotion subsides and I am left alone with Becca and she is opening my shirt, examining the wound in my side. Shortly she fetches some balm and soothes it gently into the cut, then she fastens some sort of dressing over it. Foolishly, I babble away in Spanish, asking her what has occurred, but of course she cannot answer.

Next morning, I learn the truth. A warrior comes. Gokliya has commanded my presence and I am taken to him and made to sit cross-legged.

Gokliya is not in a good mood. He reeks of tiswin. I sit quietly, having no desire to increase his ire. It is a long time before he decides to speak. When he does I am relieved to realize that his anger is not directed towards me.

'Last night,' he says, 'my word was betrayed by Soshay. I have given you safety in this place, but he attempted to kill you.'

'Why?' I gasp.

'If you were not without sight, I would call you a fool. It is evident to all that he believes Becca to be his woman. He disregards the fact that she was unfaithful to her previous husband; he disregards her disfigurement. But she turns her back on him, caring only for you. That is why he tried to kill you.'

I do not answer. I do not know what to say.

'It was not right that he should try to kill you while you slept,' Gokliya continues, 'but I understand his feelings. He says he is sorry for what he did, but he still wishes to fight you. He wants to fight you with knives.'

Knives! His words seep into my brain. I feel dazed. At last I speak.

'I would gladly fight him, but I cannot see.'

He grunts contemptuously.

'Soshay will not see either. He will be blind-folded.'

★ ★ ★

I have no experience in knife-fighting, though instinct will have me slashing from side to side. I console myself with the thought that whilst I have never fought with a blade, my opponent is equally inexperienced in coping with blindness. Perhaps our two different deficiencies will combine to make this a more even conflict. But I am not hopeful. Already I can feel sweat moistening my body, streaming down my back and buttocks.

For a moment, I recall Becca pleading with me in her unintelligible words, her arms about me, her pliant body pressed against mine, her tears wetting my face. Unintelligible her words may be, but her sentiments are universal. *Do not fight him, Webster. He will kill you.*

At one time I might not have believed that I was her suitor, but I have overlooked that she was *my* suitor. But now my feelings for her are as profound as hers are for me. And one thing is certain. I will fight for her to the death.

With my fingers I feel the knife I have been given. The blade seems to be about eight inches long and is double-edged at the point. The handle is thick and fashioned from wood bound with thong. It is what men call a 'Bowie knife'. No doubt Soshay has a similarly vicious weapon and right now is champing at the bit for the fight to commence.

A knife is not a white man's weapon, but I was offered no choice.

There can be few less enviable situations. I am trapped within a circle of Indians who are shouting like spectators at a cockfight, shouting for my blood. Strangely, I do not feel afraid at this moment. I have learned that fear usually comes after the event, and it may well be that, for me, there will be no afterwards.

Gokliya seems to be taking a neutral attitude in the whole affair, anxious to see that justice is done, though no doubt enjoying in anticipation the forthcoming spectacle of two men, rendered equally sightless, striving to disembowel each other. It will be an unusual diversion, even by Apache standards.

I have been stripped naked, as I presume has been Soshay. I have worked my muscles since dawn to make them supple. At this moment, there will be nothing Soshay wants more than to regain some esteem within the tribe by dispatching me in spectacular fashion. Perhaps by cutting my heart out and holding it up. He will then reclaim Becca, who will have no option but to become his woman. The thought angers me. I feel deeply indebted to her, and utterly compelled to protect her from this man whom she obviously does not love.

I have a mouth filled with bile. I swallow. I flex my arms, my hands.

'Fight!' It is Gokliya's voice that cuts into the babble; one sharp word that no doubt will send either Soshay or myself sliding towards an agonizing death.

My fingers tighten on the Bowie haft. For a moment, I stand quite still, poised on the balls of my feet, my body somehow drawn inward to reduce its target area. I feel a conspiracy of many against me; it is like an impact upon my brow. But I remember advice Old Santo once gave me. *A divided self is no self*. I struggle to find the hard bright grain of my own volition. Without this mastery I cannot hope to master my enemy. I strive to catch any sound that may reveal Soshay's proximity, but the shouting of the surrounding mob blankets everything, the unrestrained jeers of people in whom cruelty is a bottomless pit.

I imagine that Soshay is groping his way across the space that separates us, his knife jabbing forward — and a hideous thought hits me. Supposing he has eased the blindfold away from his eyes, even slightly. This will give him overwhelming advantage. Who is there to ensure fair play? Nobody, except Gokliya himself who is probably too drunk on tiswin to pay close attention.

As I force my feet into action, stepping forward, Soshay hits me like a stampeding buffalo, slamming me backwards into the crowding mob who immediately thrust me once more into my opponent's way. I am still gasping for breath as his hands claw at me and I twist to the side, feeling the sharpness of his knife slashing my ribs. The crowd roar at what must be blood, streaming from the cut, but I am sure it is not deep. However, its pain stings me into a furious flurry of knife slashes as I strive to find him, but the blade merely slices the air, much to the mirth of those watching.

But he seems not to be so inaccurate in his attacks as I am in mine. Instinct has been raising my left arm as a shield, and I feel the cut of his blade across my biceps. I stumble back, I am bleeding badly — and it is then that a female voice is raised into the bedlam. The words, I cannot understand, but the effect is instantaneous. A hush sweeps over the mob.

I realize that it is Becca who has cried out.

In Spanish, Gokliya tells Soshay to hold back, that his blindfold has slipped away from his eyes and the fight must not be recommenced until it is fastened. Now, in the silence, I sense that somebody has stepped into the ring to attend to the blindfold, and as I hear the satisfied grunt of his voice I am able to gauge Soshay's position.

Gokliya shouts for the fight to continue and I immediately drop on to my haunches, bracing myself against the ground.

Exerting my full force, I launch myself, knife raised, hunched side and buttock in the direction of my enemy. This time I am lucky. He cries out with shock as my knife jabs into his flesh, embedded so deeply that I cannot draw it out. He emits a high-pitched, gurgling groan and I lunge towards the sound, swinging my fists, missing twice, but on the third occasion catching him, I'm certain, in the kidney region. I feel the burn of his frothing rage. His knife clatters to the ground, and now I am fully aware of his position. It is almost as if I can see him.

I claw at him like a bob-cat, seize the flesh of his shoulder and hang on, my teeth burying themselves in his upper arm. He is grunting, snarling — but he is weakening. As he rips himself clear, I swing my fist, connect solidly and hear the bones of his nose break. He goes down, and in my frenzy, I stumble over his body and go down myself, my breath rasping from lungs worked to desperation. I scramble to him, get my hands around his throat, thumbs to his windpipe, ram his head against the ground, once, twice, three times. But then my hands, slippery with sweat and blood, lose their grip and I roll clear.

The surrounding noise is pandemonium. I am sprawled, seeking communion with the earth, feeling sure that I will present a lesser target should my assailant attempt further aggression. If he does, I know I will offer little defence. I am utterly spent. I can feel blood ebbing from my wounds, more grievously than I had at first imagined. And suddenly I hear Becca's voice at my side and she embraces me, her hair soft and cool against my sweating face.

'Soshay is dead,' Gokliya is saying.

'The fight was fair. Now it is over and finished.'

The mob is crowding about us. I yearn for cool air.

My head is filled with a red vapour, but now I am beyond caring. I have survived a monumental challenge. I have proved the inner strength of my soul, what Gokliya calls 'my power'.

10

Apache law is ruthless and clean-cut. It is applied with no uncertain stroke. My difference with Soshay is settled. I have risen instead of falling, and I have earned my victory. But I do not feel exultant.

A day, or perhaps two, passes. Gokliya comes to me and I am thankful that his voice is no longer angry. He enquires of my wounds and I tell him that Becca has cared for them well and I am healing.

'Webster,' he says, 'you cannot stay here.'

'I will gladly depart,' I say. 'You have been good to me and so has Becca. I cannot see her but I know she is a good woman and I wish I could repay her. I wish to return to the United States but it is a long way and I cannot travel alone.'

'I understand what you say,' he says, 'but I cannot spare any of my warriors to guide you back. Soshay has gone. We are few already. Perhaps I could spare somebody to take you to a Mexican town. But gringos are not popular. They hate them almost as much as they do Apaches.'

'I need to cross the border,' I say. 'There are men waiting there, men who will come to destroy Escobedo. That will be good for Apaches as well as White-Eyes.'

He does not answer.

After a moment I speak the only words that come into my head. 'Like Gokliya, I have great inner power. I have set my mind on getting revenge for the killing of my brother. Since I was made blind, the gods have always favoured me, always opened a door when all appeared lost. If one of your warriors will guide me to Maverick Springs, I will find a way. Remember, I have a secret power, like Gokliya.'

He laughs. It is good to hear him laughing again.

'I like crazy people,' he says. I reach out, feel his leathery hand grasp mine in a long shake. 'Yes, Webster, you should have been an Apache. I will find somebody to guide you across the border.'

'When?' I ask. The fear is in me that already Carleton's men, waiting in Maverick Springs, will have grown impatient and left.

'Tomorrow, maybe. Becca will take you.'

'Oh,' I murmur. I am surprised but inwardly I am rejoicing.

'Webster,' he says, 'let us sweat together and say prayers for good things.'

I nod apprehensively.

★　★　★

The sweat lodge is near a stream. Gokliya leads me to it in the evening. I touch it. It is fashioned from willow branches and covered with earth, no doubt to make it as airtight as possible.

Also present are several other warriors. As we strip naked, I cause some laughter. One of my companions says my skin is so white it hurts his eyes.

I am led inside and we squat down. I hear a splashing sound, and realize that water is being sprinkled on heated rocks. It produces an almost deafening hissing of steam. It becomes so hot within the lodge that I imagine I am suffocating or being boiled alive. Am I falling foul of some deadly Apache trick? I am tempted to run from the place, but am conscious that my companions are bearing it. I grit my teeth and am determined not to let my panic show. I draw scorching, steamy air into my lungs. Amazingly, I survive. Presently, Gokliya recites prayers to Yusn. His voice seems muffled by the steam, as if coming from a distance. I cannot understand the prayer. Meanwhile more water is thrown on the rocks.

It seems a lifetime that we sweat together.

That night when I take to my pallet, I have never felt such bodily cleanliness. I am sapped and weary, yet immensely fulfilled.

★　★　★

I awake suddenly, feeling Becca's hand on my shoulder. I start to speak, but she hushes me, and we listen together.

Hoofs are drumming upon the ground. Dogs have set up a barking frenzy. A man screams out, '*Rurales!*' and I feel Becca shudder with fear. I too am apprehensive. *Rurales . . . Rurales!* These are Mexican irregulars, most of them killers and bandits released from prison, as bloodthirsty as any Indians, ill-disciplined yet steadfast to comply with their orders to destroy Apaches. And if Apache scalps can be taken for prize money, so much the better.

Immediately a volley of gunfire erupts and I can hear much scurrying amid the wickiups. Women are screaming, dogs barking. Becca urges me to my feet and I grab my coat because that is where I conceal my Derringer and I may need it soon. The gunfire is rising in intensity as I am hastened through the wickiup entrance, not stopping even to gather my boots. The air about us seems vibrant with bullets and the smell of cordite makes us cough. I have experienced it before. There is much rushing around us, much shouting, screaming. We stumble into hurrying people — Apache women and children I am sure, but nobody stops. It is a moment of extreme danger, no doubt.

But my indomitable Becca is not deterred, her grip remains tight on my arm. On her tongue, my name seems to fulfil the purpose of all words . . . 'Webster . . . Webster!'

I push myself with all possible haste, for I know that any delay will not only endanger myself, but her as well.

Entwined with the roar of gunfire, I now hear the crackle of flames, licking through the wickiups, and with it the pungent smell of smoke that thickens the air and cuts into the throat. I can feel the heat on my back and wonder if Apache women and children are perishing, burned to death in their homes. Are Apache scalps being taken for financial reward? What had been a haven of tranquillity, albeit transient, has changed into a cauldron of violence.

The air takes on the redolence of horse flesh and manure. We have reached the remuda. Animals are stomping and whinnying at the proximity of gunshots and flames, but Becca guides me to a particular animal — it is Patience, and he is already saddled. Becca must have been preparing for our departure before the attack came.

I calm Patience, haul myself into the saddle and ram my toes into the stirrups. Becca has mounted another animal alongside me, grasping a halter attached to Patience's muzzle. Straight away, she is leading the way clear of the remuda along a winding, rising trail. We gather speed. All I can do is hunch low in the saddle, cling on, and trust Becca and Patience. Several times I am almost thrown off as we cover rugged ground, but somehow I hold on, and gradually the sound of battle behind us is growing fainter. We do not relent, galloping on, sometimes scraping foliage as we progress. Presently we splash across a shallow stream but do not pause.

I wonder what has befallen Gokliya and his people. Why were they so unprepared for surprise attack in their secluded rancheria? Could they have been betrayed? And are Becca and I now safe from immediate danger?

If we are, Becca is taking no chances. For what seems an eternity, our pace continues, an unrelenting, hammering stride, until are animals are slick with lather and I feel flecks of foam striking my face. Only then do we pause and behind us all the confusion and noise from the rancheria have been absorbed by the night. It is as if it were a horrific dream.

Throughout what is left of the night,

we ride and rest, ride and rest.

The calmness has returned to me, the odd detachment from any perils that lie ahead, and I feel a warm enchantment with my companion. While there are still few words between us beyond our names, she is not silent. She talks away in her own tongue. She seems to know the country well, and Patience remains sure-footed, faithfully following the other horse. Presently, as we stop yet again, birds are calling and I sense that it is daybreak. Becca encourages me to dismount and we refresh ourselves in a stream. She produces pemmican, having prepared for our departure even before it was hastened by the attack of *rurales*. Pemmican consists of dried meat, pounded into powder and mixed with melted fat and wild berries. As we eat, I conclude that no military banquet which I have attended ever provided tastier fare.

We move on again and I wonder where we are going. Presently, I say:

'We go to Maverick Springs?'

Her tone reflects the affirmative. 'Mav-ereek Spring.'

At noon we stop for a siesta.

This place is pleasantly shaded, a haven where the ground is softened by pine needles and songbirds serenade us.

Becca spreads a blanket, and as we rest together, she soothes my face with her fingers, then her lips touch my eyelids and she traces little kisses across them. For a while I wonder if such tenderness will restore my sight. But as the darkness remains, I seek solace with her touch.

Presently, she guides my fingers across her face, to her nose, and for the first time I become aware of her disfigurement. Half her nose seems to be missing, the nostrils unnaturally high, the flesh flattened and rough. For a moment I am puzzled, then I realize what she is telling me. She is baring her soul to me, confessing her past, confessing her ugliness.

I recall how Gokliya mentioned her

infidelity to her husband. I also recall the barbaric custom of the Apache towards a woman caught in adultery — the mutilation of the nose, so that all will know her shame.

I notice her sudden stillness. She is awaiting my reaction. I draw her to me and kiss her. To me, she is the most beautiful creature in the world.

'Webster,' she murmurs, savouring my name. 'Webster.'

She has bared her breasts and now she draws my hands to them, and I can feel how the nipples have hardened. The blood is pounding in my head and there is a surge within my loins and I know that my long period of chastity, somehow enforced by disability and grief, is ended. I do not care about Becca's past, that we come from different worlds. We share some inner feeling, some depthless, almost feral, affinity that overwhelms all else.

I feel the strength, the pliability in her body, and my desire is mixed with gratitude for all she has done for me and it is a sweet feeling. I caress her, find the moist softness of her secret place, and listen to the sounds she emits, the panting that flutters somewhere in her throat. Our taste, touch and smell become mingled to an extreme that bonds us. I slide into her, and, in our oneness, we are escaping into a world of soaring rapture where the past and everything that lies within the future no longer exists.

Later, she curls up in my arms and I softly sing *Little Brown Jug* and *Bonny Jean* and she sleeps like a happily tired puppy.

★   ★   ★

I know that my relationship with this Apache girl is drawing me deep towards lasting entrustment. She is my good luck, my fortune. Despite her kindness and compassion, she will expect a price to be paid. That price will be commitment. She would not be human if that were not the case. But I feel like flotsam, adrift in a hostile world, and I realize that without her, there is little hope for me. What awaits us, only God knows. Whether that god is my own Christian Almighty, or whether he be Yusn the Apache god, there is no way of telling. Perhaps they are the same, who knows? But there is something else. I am experiencing a sensation far more profound than anything I have previously known. I am in love. Who would dream that Lieutenant Raoul Webster of the United States Cavalry, the pride of his regiment and of his father, would give his heart to a wild Indian girl and not miss for a second the vanity, the capriciousness, the coquetry of a *Yanqui* girl?

Now we are riding on, resting at noon, travelling mostly in the early morning and late evening. Becca has made me a pair of simple moccasins, fashioning them with blanket and the bark of a tree, sewing them with wiry grass. They are surprisingly sturdy.

She shows the unerring trail-finding

skills that all Indians seem to possess. She is beginning to learn a few English words that I teach her, but it is difficult because I cannot see to point objects out to her and at first we are limited to definitions of feelings, particularly those of love. But she is quick to learn and each day her vocabulary and powers of expression increase.

On the third day we cross an invisible line on the land which represents the border between Mexico and Arizona. The country is the haunt of many enemies, bandits, vigilantes, scalp hunters, *rurales* and Indians, who will not appreciate our presence, but we have been fortunate for we have not been molested. Becca has watched and chosen the most concealed routes. After crossing a range of low hills and, eventually, a river, which I believe to be the Gila, we reach the small town of Maverick Springs.

I have seen many such places. They are populated by drunken, loud-mouthed oafs who boast and shoot their guns in the air while puking on their own boots. Stinking garbage litters the street.

I know that Becca is apprehensive, for if she is recognized as a hostile Apache woman, she will be seen not as a person, but as a creature whose scalp will fetch blood-money. However, I tell her to lift her blanket over her head, to cling to my arm, and to let me know immediately anybody shows an unhealthy interest in us. I try to remind her that there are many Indians of other tribes who frequent such settlements and are not maltreated, and she shows courage, though I doubt she understands what I am saying.

We ride into the main street and I can hear people talking on the side-walks. Presently, the tinkle of a piano and the clink of glasses sound. Some-how, we have located the saloon. We dismount and hitch our animals to a rail. Becca grasps my arm and I can feel the tremble in her. I doubt that she has ever been in a White-Eye town before. Previously, such places would have meant death to her, and now . . . what has changed? We push aside the batwings of the entrance, step inside. There is an overwhelming smell of stale liquor, smoke and even the taint of cheap perfume. In the background, the jingle of the piano continues for a few seconds, then stops. *Oh Susanna!* The place is not overcrowded, but I note the sudden quiet at our entry. As Becca guides me towards the bar, somebody shouts out, 'Injun scum ain't allowed in here! It's against the law,' and a few voices mumble agreement.

I pull up, holding Becca close. She is as tense as a bow spring.

'I am blind,' I say. 'She guides me.'

Again there comes a sort of stunned silence, then the original speaker curses and says:

'Well, don't linger any longer than you have to, mister.'

Not for the first time I appreciate the occasional advantage my disability affords.

I nudge Becca and we move to the

bar, and the barman says, 'No drinks for Injuns, but what can I do for you, sir?'

'I've come here to meet a man,' I say. 'His name's Louis Dupont. He's expecting me.'

'Oh, that damn Frenchman. He's most likely over at the hotel. You find yourself a seat. Best place'll be on the veranda outside. I'll send somebody over to fetch Dupont. He and his crew've been kicking their heels round here for weeks. We don't need the likes of them in town.'

I hear liquid being poured into a glass and he says, 'Have a beer on the house, take it outside and keep out of trouble.'

I nod my thanks.

Shortly Becca and I are seated at an outside table where the atmosphere is less intimidating.

Ten minutes later I meet for the first time Louis Dupont, the man whom Edwin Carleton has hired to ride into Mexico and rescue his daughter. He was recommended by Jonas Simpson, which, in my mind, immediately places his reputation in doubt. He is the leader of six men who will be paid by Carleton if they achieve success.

Dupont shakes my hand with a firmness that is cruel. He shows little sorrow as I explain that Simpson is dead. He seems more concerned with the boredom he and his gang have suffered.

'We waited 'ere so long, *monsieur*, we figured both of you were dead. Seemed a crazy idea anyway, sending a blind man to find Gokliya. We thought it was a joke. But the good thing is that Carleton is paying us for our time. If it 'adn't been for that, we'd 'ave gone 'ome ages ago.'

'I was delayed by events,' I explain.

He grunts his acknowledgement, then says, 'That woman of yours is Apache. Apache scalps are worth good money.'

'She's not Apache,' I lie. 'She is Navajo, and I'll kill anybody who harms a single strand of her hair.'

He laughs at my threat. 'I know she is Apache,' he says. 'Only Apaches cut off a woman's nose when she unfaithful. She cannot conceal what she is, no matter 'ow much you lie.' I feel his breath upon my face as he leans forward. 'The most important thing is,' he goes on, ' 'ave you found out who kidnapped Carleton's daughter, and where she's held? I 'ope that little minx is worth all the trouble 'er father is going to to get 'er back.'

I nod towards Becca and say, 'She knows where the Mexican bandits have their hideaway. She'll guide us there, but she does not speak English or Spanish.'

'Well, that's as good as any reason for keeping her alive, at least until we get there.' He hesitates, then says, 'You said she'll show 'us', *monsieur*. You are not figuring on coming along, are you?'

'Yes,' I respond. 'I have unfinished work to attend to concerning the murder of my brother. Becca will make sure I don't slow you down.'

'Well, I do not know,' he grumbles.

'I'm coming,' I say, and he does not argue any more. No doubt he figures I will be as easily disposed of as the girl if I get troublesome.

In the afternoon, I purchase a new pair of boots.

That evening we meet Dupont's crew. They scoff at me and say that I am as blind as a post hole, and couldn't hit a bull's ass with a handful of banjos. In truth they are nothing more than hired gunmen, *pistoleros*, riff-raff of the border country. From what I can gather, they are mostly Texans, and all used to operating outside the law. No law-abiding citizens would risk going into another country without government blessing. There are no formal introductions, but what I sense is that they are highly dangerous men, and totally uncouth in their foul manners and behaviour. If Becca could understand English, I would caution them to watch their language.

I remind myself that the girl is important to them because of her knowledge of the location of Escobedo's hacienda. As for myself, they might tolerate my presence for a while, but if the whim takes them, they can shoot me in an instant and few people would be any the wiser. But I steel myself for the challenges ahead — and realize how dependent I am on my Apache lover. She is immensely brave and I am determined that she must come to no harm.

11

It is strange. The closer I get to the one who took James's life, the closer I feel to my brother. It is almost as if he is riding alongside Becca and me, joining us to avenge his killing. Sometimes I seem to hear the ripple of his laugh or, in my mind, see the white flash of his teeth. I recall the way we would climb trees, splash in the stream behind our house, gallop our ponies in the meadow. He made little fuss over his crippled leg, always striving to achieve greater heights than those with sound limbs, as if to prove something to the world. Now, he lingers in my mind increasingly. It is as if he is more alive than ever he was in true life. I think he is part of my power, just as Becca is.

A Texan called Jug appears to be second-in-command of this gang of cutthroats. Why he is called Jug, I cannot imagine, but his name sticks in my mind. Another man is called Kelvin, and he has a cough so bad that it makes phlegm rattle like pebbles in his chest. The names of the others have become familiar to me — One Eye, Willard, Fraser. I have got to differentiate between them by the jingle of their spurs, all of which are slightly varied.

Over the days ahead, it is in their unpredictable company that Becca leads the way back into Mexico, the homeland of Jesus Escobedo.

⋆ ⋆ ⋆

Jug and Dupont have left the rest of us a couple of miles from Escobedo's hacienda. They have gone to spy on it.

I know that this is a particularly dangerous time, for neither my own presence nor Becca's is required any longer — but if any of our companions have considered disposing of us, we have not been threatened so far. At present, the four men left behind are gathered around a camp-fire. I believe they are playing some sort of card-game.

I wonder about the girl, Gabriella Carleton. Is she still alive? *She is pretty. Her hair is as black as ebony*, James told me. I recall the softness of her Louisiana voice. Has she been violated, the victim of lust, her young body explored, her intimacy exposed and mutilated by cruel hands? My mind is full of questions. They sit uneasily atop my unremitting anger. I have no answers. Only one thing is certain: I hate Escobedo, no matter what he has, or has not, done.

We have made camp amid some trees, and when I feel the wedge-shaped, hairy leaves and scaly bark, I conclude that they are smokethorn. I wonder if Escobedo is at home, or is he away, inflicting his violence, his murder, on some other unsuspecting victims? Perhaps he is out hunting for Apache scalps — even Gokliya's. What a prize that would be, worth far more than the standard two hundred pesos offered by the Mexican government.

Becca senses my anguish and whispers soothing words in my ear. We sit close, her slim hand resting on mine as we listen to the shrill calls of swifts and the soft chunking sound of the horses as they pull at grassy stems. Presently, I hear Becca whispering words softly to herself. It is some sort of chant, perhaps a prayer to her own god, Yusn.

Some yards off, the men of Dupont's gang have built a small fire, and the welcome aroma of coffee wafts to us on the air. I do not trust these men and I know that Becca is equally apprehensive. They will be totally unscrupulous if put to the test, and I say my own prayer that matters will be drawn to a satisfactory conclusion before relationships are strained to breaking-point. Meanwhile, I must bide my time and do my utmost to avoid stretching their patience. I wish some plan of action would form in my mind, but there is nothing.

Presently, I remove my Derringer pistol from my coat pocket, clean it, oil it and ensure that it is properly loaded. I wish it was more than a single-shot, but a bigger weapon would be too cumbersome for me. Should I ever need it, there will be no time for a misfire. I can reload it, but it would be a slow process. I replace it carefully in the pocket.

Just before nightfall, we hear the sound of approaching horsemen and we realize that Dupont and Kelvin are returning from their scouting trip. Soon their voices are raised in conversation and I edge closer to pick up their words. Sure enough, they have located the hacienda, but apparently the gates stand open and everywhere is surprisingly quiet. They crept in close and jumped upon a one-armed peon working in the fields. Firstly, they had kicked him into submission. Under threat of a slit throat the man revealed that Escobedo and his men were not in residence, but had ridden out yesterday.

They were going to recover the *Yanqui* girl Gabriella Carleton, who had previously escaped. She, apparently, had been recaptured by a friend of Escobedo. I hear all this as I crouch down close to the camp-fire with my ears pinned back.

The news is interesting. It indicates that Gabriella may still be alive, and also suggests a reason why the ransom has not been demanded from Edwin Carleton. The girl has obviously been more of a handful than her captors had expected and somehow gave Escobedo the slip, at least for a while.

Now I listen as Louis Dupont is outlining a plan. He has spied out the road that leads to the hacienda, seen how at one point it passes through a narrow canyon. Escobedo and his men are bound to return by this route, and in so doing will place themselves in an ideal place to be ambushed. A volley of well-directed shots from behind the cover of the overhanging rim would cut them down as easily as shooting fish in a barrel. Or so my companions seem to think. Of course the unknown factor is: when will Escobedo and his bandits return? It could be within hours, days or weeks — but Dupont is intent on proceeding with his plan of ambush. I wonder, if Escobedo has recovered the girl, how she will survive the hail of bullets if the ambush takes place at the canyon, but this appears not to concern Dupont or his cronies. At any rate, I can think of no better plan than his and I am determined to keep track of events as best I can.

Dupont is concerned that the Mexicans may slip through the canyon at any time, or indeed may already have done so.

Without delay we saddle our horses and ride out. As we progress, I hear owls hooting on the cool breeze and I conclude that it is night. As usual, Becca leads my horse with a hackamore halter, and Dupont is making no concessions, for we jolt along at a brisk clip over uneven ground.

* * *

I have difficulty in measuring the passage of time, but it seems much later that Dupont calls a halt and our group reins in. We all dismount, glad enough to stretch our legs. Becca hugs close to me as Dupont launches into conversation with his men. They keep their voices low, but my conclusion is that there is no indication that Escobedo and his gang have passed through. Presently, we set up cold camp and I gather that Dupont sets a guard to watch the canyon. Becca and I are left to our own devices, but there is little we can do but squat upon the rocks and wait for time to pass. I feel Becca's head nestle into my shoulder, and her closeness is comforting. After a while, her breathing changes and I know that she is sleeping. I also know that the slightest disturbance or noise will rouse her instantly.

The hours of the day stretch away. We eat, drink coffee, wait . . . Dupont's motley crew squabble amongst themselves, swapping crude jokes, sometimes playing cards, I guess. I sense that Dupont keeps his distance from them, and that they hold him in awe, for they never argue with him and seem to scurry quickly to fulfil his orders. He is like his fellow countryman Napoleon Bonaparte and keeps aloof from his subordinates.

Dupont changes his guards several times and each reports back that there is no movement along the canyon. Dawn comes and the heat starts to build. The Mexicans could return within minutes, hours, days, weeks — or never. I wonder how long Dupont's patience will stretch.

Becca and I attend to our horses. I am immensely grateful for her presence and help and eventually conclude that if I have to be bored, I would sooner be bored with her as my companion than anybody else in the entire world. Sometimes we laugh together at things that seem inconsequential, like when I reach out and, inadvertently, touch her where no true gentleman would touch a lady. It is strange how, deep down, people are the same regardless of whether they are white or Indian. Eventually I conclude that she likes to be touched by me, no matter where.

It will seem incredible that we waited on the ridge overlooking that canyon for almost a week. From what I can understand, a coach passed along the road, as did a number of peons driving carts — but there was no sign of Escobedo.

I think it is on the sixth night of our wait that I am suddenly awakened. I can hear Becca's panting breath. It comes with the frenzy shown by a woman in childbirth. For a moment, I strive to comprehend what is happening, then I hear the grunt of a man and I shout out. Immediately, I hear the scrape of boots coming across the rock and Dupont's voice comes:

'I told you not to touch the girl!'

There is no time for any response.

140

The vicious blast of his pistol shatters the night. I crouch, feeling sweat moisten my body, the smell of gunpowder in my nostrils. As the echo of the shot fades, I am aware of Becca's low moaning sound. I reach out and her hand slips into mine.

' 'E will not trouble you again,' Dupont says, and then he speaks to his men, 'Get rid of the body.'

I clutch on to Becca, feeling the shudder in her subside. I curse myself for not being able to protect her more adequately — but I feel perhaps I have misjudged Louis Dupont. Maybe he is not the enemy I have imagined, but a protector. A rough diamond. I am quite sure that without him Becca and I would have been dead as soon as the location of the hacienda was discovered. But I censure myself. Even a rattlesnake has its soft underbelly.

The following day, there is less levity among the remaining gang. No joshing, no crude humour. The only sound I hear is the ceaseless coughing of

Kelvin. The foolishness of crossing their leader has been truly demonstrated.

It is evening when at last Jug calls out from his viewpoint:

'*The Mexicans. They're comin' along the trail!*'

* ★ ★ ★

There is immediate scurrying about me. I hear the hiss of the camp-fire as it is doused with water. Dupont issues orders in a rapid, hushed voice, and there is the muted, metallic sound of firearms being cocked, followed by the almost inaudible scrape of boots across the rocks. I know that Dupont has already drawn up plans of where each man will position himself to the greatest advantage. Becca draws me back into some nearby boulders and we crouch down, our breathing restrained as we listen. There is nothing we can do at this moment but take cover and pray that whatever outcome emerges from the intended ambush will favour us.

It seems an eternity that we wait. It is a period of time when the lives of men await their termination. Becca and I are completely alone, our presence momentarily of no consequence to Dupont's men. Utter silence dominates. It is as deep as the grave. The air is cool on my face. I clutch Becca's hand tightly, steady myself and allow myself to breathe calmly. The silence continues, and I wonder if it has been some sort of false alarm — perhaps a mirage that appeared as approaching riders, but in truth was nothing more than shimmering cactus. But I remind myself that the sun has gone from the day, that now is not the time for mirages.

And then the murmur of voices drifts up from the canyon — Mexican voices, and even the grunt of laughter, and simultaneously the clop of hoofs sound on the rocky trail. Clip clop, clip clop ... is Dupont delaying for too long! I feel a pulse pounding in my temple, a sweat of anticipation beading out on me. I have waited months for this moment. I wonder if Escobedo is down there in the canyon, blissfully unaware that his evil ways are about to be punished by execution. I would have chosen for him a slow death, perhaps the way the Apaches would have administered it — but the matter has been taken out of my hands. All I can do is rely on the accurate fire of Dupont's men.

I slip my arm around Becca, hug her to me: I can feel her heart beating against my chest, smell the scent of her hair. It matters not to me whether her face has been made ugly. I know that her spirit is beautiful.

And then Dupont's voice yells an order and the crash of gunfire erupts!

It bludgeons our eardrums, seeming louder than all the thunder in heaven, making Becca and me draw so close that we are as one person, in a world apart from that where men are dying. Intermingled with the gunfire comes the awful shocked screams of men and horses. Time loses its exactness, seems to merge with the mixture of sounds and the acrid smell of gunpowder. It stretches into a minute, or is it an hour? Suddenly the guns die into echoing silence, broken by the groaning of men and horses. I hear Dupont shouting. He is urging his men to follow him down into the canyon, to dispatch all those who still show signs life — but even as I hear the clink of guns being recharged and the scrape of footsteps upon rock, a tremendous commotion arises.

A horse neighs wildly, then comes the drum of hoofs and guns again blast off, but the gallop of the horse continues, fading gradually into the distance. Dupont and his killers are cursing, arguing — and I know instantly that all has not gone to plan.

I hear a man's voice raised, pleading for mercy, but the pleas evoke a further gunshot and the pleas come no more. The proximity of such butchery sickens me. I swear I can smell the taint of blood, of death, in the air. But then I remind myself that any murder, any massacre, that has been inflicted, mirrors that which the present victims perpetrated upon those travelling by stagecoach four months since. *An eye for an eye*. Perhaps even this fate is too good for them, but it is what I have sought, dreamed of, for so long.

Even so, no sense of joy or triumph pervades me.

For a time there is the sound of movement from the canyon. The scrape of matches as torches are lit. The crack of more single shots to make certain there are no survivors. Then I hear Louis Dupont issuing orders for the bodies to be dragged to the side of the trail, signs of the ambush, as much as possible, to be erased.

It is only when Dupont eventually climbs out of the canyon and approaches us that I call out to him.

'Escobedo . . . have you killed him?'

He curses in French, long and hard. 'No, *mon ami*. Escobedo got away. 'E and one other, riding a single horse. We had no 'orses down there, so we could not give chase.'

'Then you will follow his trail,' I say, 'track him down, finish the job?'

'When it is daylight. With your blind eyes you cannot see that the night has come. We will pick up 'is trail at dawn.'

'And Carleton's daughter? What has happened to her?'

'*Je ne sais pas*. We found no sign of 'er.'

It is my turn to curse. Come daylight, the killer of my brother, the abductor, could be miles away.

12

This night drags interminably. I cannot rest, but lie feeling the cold air wash across my face. We remain at our camp above the canyon, the canyon that has become a resting-place for the dead. I am conscious that each passing second probably means that Escobedo is further away. Dupont has emphasized my own opinion that having lost so many of his men (Dupont says he has counted ten bodies), he will not dare return to his hacienda. It would be too easy for those seeking him to trap him there. Instead he will ride deeper into these, his homeland mountains, which no doubt he knows better than even the Apaches.

I listen to the sounds of the night — the gentle murmur of Becca's breathing, the intermittent howling of a coyote and the yip-yapping response, the hooting of an owl, the scurrying of mice and lizards. I am impatient for time to pass, but I know Dupont is right. Come daylight, across the rocks, it will be difficult to find Escobedo's tracks, but in the present darkness it would be impossible, and in our haste we might end up miles from our prey.

At last, I imagine that dawn must be edging the distant mountains with its first light. I hear the murmur of quail, sense a slight change in the temperature, and within minutes I hear Dupont rousing his men with French profanity. Becca has long been awake, and soon she is on her feet, completing the tasks that are necessary to start the new day, both for herself and me.

I know we are like parasites to the gang. We are nothing more than an encumbrance. To them, it will not matter whether we keep up or drag behind. As always, I must rely on Becca to lead me, following the others, no matter how fast they ride.

After a quick sup of coffee, we walk

to the grassy swale where our horses have been left and saddle them quickly. Once mounted up, the party rides out, Becca and I trailing along as inconspicuously as possible. Mesquite has dropped its peapod summer beans onto the rock and these crunch noisily beneath the horses' hoofs.

Presently, from the snatches of conversation that drift back to me, I understand that we have returned to the canyon, and there we rein in — and soon I can hear the buzz of myriads of flies no doubt drawn by the corpses, both human and equine, piled at the side of the trail.

Dupont calls that he has found the hoof marks of Escobedo's desperate flight, and with grunts of satisfaction all around, we are once again on the move. We follow the trail for perhaps a mile, then swing off into rougher country. At West Point I was taught the rudiments of tracks: the passage through grass, the examination of horse-dung dropped, the position of a mount's feet to indicate speed and direction. Now, sadly, I can only rely on the sight of others to follow the trail, but it seems that Dupont and Jug are experts.

But all the expertise in the world cannot stave off the disaster that now strikes.

The shot, when it comes, awakes a mass of echoes from the adjacent rock faces and sends swarms of birds up in squawking flight. The men around me are suddenly shouting with alarm and horses are whinnying and rearing. By the time the second shot comes, Becca has clawed on to my leg, has dragged me from the saddle. I land awkwardly, but as she draws me scurryingly to the close-by rocks, I suspect that she has saved my life, not for the first time.

I hear Jug shouting: 'Where the hell is he!'

'High up on the cliff,' another man responds, and there follows a fusillade of shots. This soon stops, and in the sudden hush I become aware of my companions cursing.

'Whoever it was has high-tailed by now, that's for sure.'

'It was Escobedo, no doubt.'

'Gone blown Dupont's brains out!' somebody remarks and I groan. I feel as if a trapdoor has opened beneath me, leaving me dangling in a situation as fragile as a spider's web. Maybe Dupont has never been a friend, but it was he who protected Becca and me from the violence of his men. Without him only Becca can watch them, bring warning of their intent.

For a moment it seems all they can do is curse over and over. I hear them moving around and Jug says, 'Let's round up the horses.'

Another man says, 'I don't fancy this. Escobedo can take a pot shot any time he chooses. Pick us off one by one.'

'Well, let's get movin',' Jug retorts. 'Ain't no point in hangin' around here.'

'We can't just leave Dupont for the buzzards!'

'Yes we can,' Jug says. 'We're sittin' ducks while we stay round here.'

There was a general grunting of agreement.

I feel Becca squeeze my fingers. It is a familiar signal. It means, 'Wait!' and she moves away from me. I crouch where I am. I worry about her. Any time Escobedo might strike again — and this time his bullet might find her. I groan at the thought, but minutes later she is back with both her own mount and Patience. She is my worker of miracles.

Around us, the others are talking. Their voices are low and uneasy, lacking the usual arrogance.

'I guess we better head for the hills to the east,' Jug says, 'then circle around and see if we can pick up his trail again.'

'Well I figure the best thing we can do is get the hell out o' here. This country's just ideal for bushwhacking. I don't figure on gettin' my brains blowed out. I don't give a damn about Carleton's money!'

'I agree. Can't spend no money if'n you're dead.'

'Now listen here,' Jug counters. 'Just 'cos Louis is killed don't mean we gotta give up. I guess those of you who want to turn back had better go, but don't expect any share of the spoils. I'm goin' on and those of you who want to come with me better make your minds up quick. I guess we best spread out, make less of a target that way.'

'Well, I don't know . . . '

'I'm with you, Jug.' It is Kelvin's voice and is followed by the usual cough.

Their uncertainty flows about me like flood-water. Nobody asks my opinion. If they asked me, I'd would say, 'Let's go on. We haven't come all this way to get sidetracked.' But nobody cares what I think. I am totally irrelevant to them — and as for Becca: sooner or later they will remember that she is Apache, that her scalp is worth good money.

I should give such matters thought, balance the risks in going on against sanity. Once in my saddle, I sit awaiting any decision that my companions may make. I do not consider that at this exact moment, my head might be aligned in the sights of Escobedo's gun, that this time his bullet might have my name on it. In the event, I give it no thought. I am blind both in my outer and inner eyes, otherwise perhaps I would realize the terrible fate that hovers over us.

I gather that no fewer than three of the surviving gang turn back. They leave without farewells, their courage having dissipated. Becca knows my own inclinations as clearly as if they are her own, for as the party splits, she jerks on the hackamore rope and Patience edges forward in the wake of Jug and Kelvin, the only two of the gang who chose to continue. They ride in silence; for once Kelvin's cough is stifled. Both men, no doubt, have their heads ducked low, their eyes on the surrounding ridges, anxious to catch the glint of morning sun on gunmetal. The day's heat is rising. Jug and Kelvin are spread apart, but not Becca and myself. I need her close to lead me. Perhaps she and I make the best target of all. Miss one, maybe, and hit the other. We ride, it seems, through an eerie, bizarre world in which the clop of our horses' hoofs is awesomely loud, and as if all of nature is holding its breath, waiting to see what events will unfold.

At last we reach the welcome cover of timbered ground, and I guess we are circling around towards the spot from which Escobedo fired. Maybe from there Jug's keen eyes will pick up some clue as to the direction the Mexican has taken.

And thus lead us closer to our destiny.

13

I hear the subdued, nervous voices of Jug and Kelvin. Jug's words are hushed, but Kelvin's cough is raucous and loud. The clammy fear my companions feel spreads to me. I wonder how long it will be before their nerves crack and they turn back.

I know that there is so little time for reaction between the crack of a gun and the grasping claws of eternity. Escobedo could be a few feet from any of us, stepping from behind a rock, and blasting off at point-blank range before I get the slightest indication of his presence. He clearly holds the upper hand, no matter what indication of his progress Jug finds on the trail. The Mexican can play any trick he favours as he leaves his sign. He may even have doubled back. The fact that we outnumber him is of no consequence.

He can pick us off, one at a time. Perhaps he is laughing to himself as he watches from his chosen place of concealment, watches and prepares to rid himself of pursuit. He will need but four well-placed shots to finish us all.

I wonder what thoughts are in Becca's mind. She risks her life as much as any of us — with nothing for reward apart from my love. In the seemingly unlikely event of fortune smiling upon us, I am determined that our union will be sweetened by every kindness and vestige of affection I can give her. I whisper my feelings to her in English and she murmurs an acknowledgement. I hope she understands. I hope she feels a fleeting happiness. I cannot contemplate a life without her. When this is all over, I will take her East and we will build a future together, away from the constant threat of danger that is everywhere upon this wild frontier. My father will not understand how I can love a member of an alien and wild nation, but he will gradually discover the goodness in her, the sweetness of her soul.

I am conscious that Jug is progressing slowly and that we are amid redolent pine. No matter how cautiously we move, it is impossible to persuade the horses to do likewise. They snort and blow, their hoofs crackle on pine cones, and their bodies bring swishing sounds from low-hanging fronds. And then there is Kelvin's cough which he cannot seem to suppress. Unless Escobedo is far away, he is bound to be aware of our presence.

He is not far away.

The shot comes from close range with the viciousness of a whiplash snake. My companions are immediately shouting, horses whinnying, hoofs pounding as they throw themselves from their saddles. Instantaneously, they are blasting away with their own guns, the snap of their shots sounding like Chinese firecrackers.

I sit quite still upon Patience, upright in my saddle, knowing that our assailant can blast me into eternity when he chooses. But gradually the bark of guns subsides. I hear Jug shouting but cannot distinguish what he is saying beyond a string of profanity — and then my thoughts turn to Becca. I call to her, but there is no response. Panic surges through me.

'*Becca!*'

Jug's voice comes harshly. 'You can call her for as long as you like, but she ain't gonna come runnin' — not never!'

I am out of my saddle now, falling clumsily to the ground before I completely clear my foot of the stirrup. On my hands and knees I grope forward, find the hackamore limp upon the pine needles. I blunder against the legs of a horse, Becca's horse, set it rearing, feel the closeness of its stamp.

Then I find her body, touch her blood.

'Like I said,' Jug hisses, 'she won't come runnin' for you no more. Not unless you can stuff her brains back in and sew her skull back together. The pity is, her pretty Apache scalp has been blasted to bits.'

I yell with anguish.

★ ★ ★

They have left me. They showed little inclination to take me with them, but were anxious to quit this place of ambush, suspecting that Escobedo still lurked close at hand, choosing the moment for his next shot. It is a lottery in which the Mexican holds all the dice.

I have lost all concern over my fate. Any enemy can find me, be it human or wild beast, and I will not resist. I can do nothing but cradle Becca in my arms, feeling the coldness in her body, fan away the flies that come to pester. Escobedo has taken from me the two people I love the most in this life — James and Becca, and this knowledge grips my brain with the rigidity of a cruel claw, causing tears to burn my eyes and burrs to catch in my throat, and behind it all is a numbness that is oblivious to all other sensation.

I might just have well have died myself, for presently all consciousness leaves me and I spiral through darkness, falling, falling, through my sea of misery, until I remember no more.

James awakes me. He says, 'Rouse yourself, Raoul. You must go on. You must not give up now.'

His voice achieves its purpose, for I struggle into awareness. I feel the weight of Becca's body in my arms. She, like me, has grown cold, but there is a stiffness about her that makes me groan.

'Where are you, James?' I demand aloud, but he does not answer. He is not here. He has faded back into my dreams from whence he came.

I try to focus my attention on what must be done. Firstly, I am determined to place my Becca where she will be safest. I climb up, shuffle around and realize that the ground beneath my feet is soft with pine needles and humus. I sink to my knees and with bare hands start to dig. I work for what seems hours, and eventually conclude that the hole is big enough to take her precious body. I lay her to rest, crossing her stiff arms across her breasts.

I pray to both my god and Yusn that she will find the peace she so much deserves. She has died for me, just as my brother did. Now, it seems, it is only I who remain to take the long step into the next world.

I do not know how long I remain at the graveside, my head bowed, my mind clogged with grief. I am certain it is night. I wonder how far my erstwhile companions have travelled on, if indeed they still survive. Perhaps Escobedo has taken further toll. Or, alternatively, perhaps Jug has outwitted him, has inflicted on him the punishment he is due. Somehow I doubt it.

The Mexican has suffered grievous loss. He has the resourcefulness to survive us all and spend the rest of his life making others pay.

But I have an immediate problem. I

am completely lost and without sight in this vastness of the Sonora wilderness. There is nobody to help me. I am totally abandoned. I have no food, no ability to hunt, no idea which way to make progress — and I am weighed down by the grief in my heart. What hope is there for me? Am I worthy of hope, or am I to be discarded, allowed to whither to death and find my own route to the after-life?

And now it is that the sound of movement comes from behind me and my back straightens with alarm. It is a shuffling sound, growing closer. I am trembling, wondering whether it will be a bullet or a knife-blade that dispatches me.

The smell of him reaches me first, filling my nostrils with the warm, musky scent that can only mean one thing . . . *horse*!

His soft muzzle nudges my back.

I turn, embrace his head. I weep with momentary joy, feel warm tears coursing down the grime on my cheeks. I am not friendless. Patience is suddenly snorting as if he too shares my joy. I rub his withers and for a while the only sound is the soft frupping of his nostrils.

The desire to remain by Becca's grave, to protect it from wild scavengers, to commune with her spirit, tugs at me, but simultaneously I sense that she is whispering to me in words I can suddenly comprehend, the same words James has spoken. '*You must go on . . . go on.*'

I whisper a silent prayer, swearing that if I am somehow spared, I will one day return to be with her again. And if I die, I will join her in the spirit world.

The air is cool and the silence of night surrounds me. I must have been at the graveside for some hours. I grope my way alongside Patience, get my foot into the stirrup and haul myself into the saddle. A nudge of my heels has my faithful mount edging forward. Where will he take me? I suspect that even he does not know — but on we go, slowly and unconcealed. If any hidden marksman awaits us, he will have little trouble in placing his bullet. I am beyond caring. I am in the hands of Fate and of God.

We reach a stream and as Patience nose-dips and sucks up refreshment, I dismount and also drink. Every movement I make, I anticipate Becca's reassuring and guiding touch, but it does not come and the grief weighs heavily upon me, making my whole body sag under its burden. Becca, my Becca . . . dead and buried beneath pine needles. Perhaps even now the scavengers are digging for her. I shudder.

I remount the horse and we travel on. I wonder if we are moving in a useless circle. I do not know. I realize that not only am I at the mercy of Fate and God, but also of Patience. But where can he take me? Where is there to go? One thing is certain. Sooner or later I will need the help of people — be they Indian, Mexican or whatever. I try to shut my mind to the awful tragedies that have occurred, and those which wait beyond the next turn in the trail. I am lulled by the jog of the animal as he picks his way onward.

It is dawn. I hear the birds, feel the growth of an underlying warmth in the air. And suddenly I smell wood smoke, and then something even more welcome — coffee.

Patience unleashes a whinny and a response comes from horses at our front. My heart quickens, as does the horse's pace. I feel the soft scrape of trailing fronds and we emerge onto open ground.

'My God, it's our blind friend!' Jug says, and his companion says, 'Jaysus! Thought we'd left him behind for good.'

I could well reprimand them for leaving me so callously, but there is little point for they will do the same again without hesitation.

'Where's Escobedo?' I ask. 'He killed Becca. I want to find him.'

Both Jug and his companion laugh scornfully.

'You'll do a mighty lot, blind man!'

'Have you seen him since the shooting?' I persist.

Jug spits. 'We seen his blood on the ground. Figure we winged him. There's blood splashes leading up to a big cave on yonder hillside. We reckon he's gone in there. Maybe there's another way out and he's high-tailed it. He knows this country better than we do.'

'But he could still be in that cave,' I argue.

'Could be. We kept watch all night, waiting to see if he sneaked out, but he didn't.'

'Those blood splashes are maybe an attempt to lure us into a trap,' Kelvin comments. 'It's as black as a cow's belly in that cave. I ain't goin' in there to look for him.'

'He could be watching us now,' Jug says. 'Could have his gun lined up with us.'

We stand listening. Their uncertainty

hovers about us like a cloud.

'There's only one way to find out if he's in here,' Kelvin says, 'an' that's to wait till he takes a shot at us. I don't figure on being around to let him do that.'

'Carleton's payin' us good money to get Escobedo,' Jug says. 'I don't figure we should just give up.'

'Money's no good if you're dead,' Kelvin responds. 'I'm not going into that cave for all the money in the world.'

An idea grows in my mind. Some inner sense warns me that we are close to Escobedo. Perhaps he is watching us at this very moment, but I suspect that he is hiding in the black depths of the cave. The prospect of allowing him to slip away grieves me.

My voice seems to come of its own accord.

'I will go in. In the dark, Escobedo will be as blind as me. We will be on even terms. If you hear gunshots, you will know he is there.'

'That's a crazy idea,' Jug grunts impatiently. 'What good can a blind man do, 'ceptin' get himself killed?'

'You'd probably fall down some hole, break your neck!' Kelvin scoffs.

'So would you,' I say, 'in the dark. I'm more used to feeling my way around than you are.'

I know that in reality these men do not give a damn about my safety. In fact they view me as a liability. But perhaps things will change now.

'Maybe he's right,' Jug says. 'If he's willing to act as bait, I guess we would find out if that Mexican is holed up in there.'

'I need a stick,' I say. 'Find me one.'

Kelvin grunts his reluctance at obeying my order, but he moves off and I hear the snap of a branch. He soon returns and thrusts a stick into my hands. I estimate it to be about three feet long.

I untie the cotton bandanna from my neck and knot it around the end of the stick to muffle any noise.

'I'll need somebody to guide me to the entrance of the cave,' I say.

'You take him,' Jug says to Kelvin.

'Piss off!' Kelvin responds. 'You do it.'

Jug growls with anger, but his hands grip my shoulders and he turns me slightly. 'Start walking, Webster,' he says.

14

I step forward, feeling his nudge in my back. My toe catches on a rock and I stumble. I straighten up and go on. I suspect that Jug has placed me between himself and the entrance of the cave, using my frame as a shield should a bullet come. Ahead, I hear small animals scurrying out of our path, their tiny feet skittering softly on the rocks.

It takes us five minutes to reach the cave. I touch the rough surface of the wall with my hand. It is gnarled and cool in its shadow.

'This is as far as I'm goin',' Jug comments. His words somehow hang in the air. We shuffle to a halt. He gives me a firm prod and I hear him backing off, his footsteps gaining pace as they recede into the distance. Soon, he will be cowering down with Kelvin behind screening bushes, his ears pinned back for the sound of a shot which will signal my demise and the presence of Escobedo.

I probe around with my stick and discover I am standing close to the cave wall. I step forward. I sense the brooding, mausoleum-like atmosphere of the place. I am moving at a snail's pace, placing my feet with infinite care, making certain I am on firm ground before trusting it with my weight. I am particularly careful with overhead rock, for I have no wish to knock myself out. Sometimes I encounter obstructions and feel my way gingerly around them. I probe with my hands carefully, my caution increasing as I remember that snakes often nestle in the rocky crannies. None the less, I am progressing and presently I believe that I am in the deeper part of this great cavern and must certainly be concealed by the darkness. That being so, the only thing that can give my presence away is sound, and I attempt to assume the qualities of a ghost, absorbed by darkness and silence. Inside me, a voice is whispering.

Escobedo, Escobedo . . . where are you?

I pause frequently, squat down, feel around me with my hands. I imagine that I have reached some inner chamber. I am sure by now that Jug and Kelvin are concluding that the sacrificial lamb will soon be ravaged by the awaiting lion. I know that what I am doing is crazy, but no more crazy than the countless risks I have taken already. One more risk? What is the difference?

But now I cast all misgivings aside. I have more important matters to attend to. *Jesus Escobedo, killer of my beloved James, killer of sweet Becca, wrecker of my life, where are you? Don't skulk like the coward you are. Meet me on the level terms this darkness provides!*

I hold my breath, strain my senses for sound, but there is nothing, apart from the dull throb of blood in my ear drums. Not even the flapping of a bat high in the chamber roof now. It is as if the entire world is holding its breath, waiting, senses alert in fascinated awe.

I remember the knife-fight I had with Soshay. I wish I had that knife now. I grip my stick tightly. It is stout and will make a handy club, but a knife would be preferable.

I wait, motionless, perhaps as some primeval reptile did at this very spot aeons ago. To it, an hour or a year would not have been differentiated.

My nostrils widen to a familiar scent. I am puzzled, then recognition melts into my senses. It is the sour buttermilk scent of pulque, the liquor fermented from honey-water. The favored drink of many Mexicans. I remember when I smelt it before. On the breath of Escobedo just before he murdered James.

He is close by.

I must prove that my patience is greater than his. He is a hot-blooded man who, I am sure, will have but a short fuse to his Hispanic temper. How long will it be before he betrays himself?

'Why do you squat there in the light like a sitting duck?' His voice seems strangely entwined with the silence.

I am startled. I believed that I was shrouded by darkness.

'Light?' I query.

He laughs — a throaty, evil sound. 'There is a hole up there in the roof of this place, you blind fool. The light is shining down upon you. Killing you will be very easy.'

'Kill me!' I spit at him. 'Kill me like you did my brother!'

'*Mi amigo*, it will be easier than that.'

I hear the metallic click as he slides the bolt back on his gun.

'The sound of the shot will bring my friends in to get you. They weren't sure whether you were here or not. When you start shooting they will know for certain.'

Friends, I have called them. *A man would get greater support from a nest of rattlesnakes.*

'*Por amor de Dios!* I can hold them off in this place for as long as I like.'

'Yes,' I say. 'But you are already wounded. You are dying. Your blood has shown across the rocks.'

He snorts in contempt. 'Horse blood!' he grunts. 'One of your mis-aimed bullets nicked him.'

I am disappointed. I wonder if he is lying.

'There will be no escape for you,' I say. 'My friends will guard the entrance night and day, shoot you dead as soon as you appear. If you stay in here, you will starve or die of thirst. They are in no hurry. They will wait as long as is necessary. They also have the other exit guarded.'

'Other exit,' he snarls. 'There is no other exit. You are lying, blind man. You are lying in everything you say. I will kill you very soon.'

It is my turn to laugh scornfully. At least I know now that he has no means of escape other than the main entrance of the cave.

'If my friends hear a shot, they will know you are here,' I tell him.

'As gringos say, there are many ways to skin a cat,' he says. 'There are also many ways to kill a blind man.'

Of course he is right, but we are playing a game.

'You know,' he says, 'all this trouble need never have happened. It was not our intention to kill anybody when we held up the coach. All we wanted was the girl. It was the driver and guard who started the shooting. All we did was retaliate.'

'Why did you want the girl?' I ask.

I hear him sigh deeply. 'Her father is an incredibly rich man. He could afford to get her back.'

'Then why didn't you demand a ransom?'

He emits a low growl, like an angry animal. 'She escaped. The little vixen tricked her guard and ran off.'

'And why did you kill my brother?' I demand.

'We thought he had a gun.'

'He was unarmed and had a crippled leg.'

'Then that was his bad luck. He should have stayed at home. And so should you. At least we spared you. If you had any sense, you'd have stayed where you were safe. Where there was somebody to guide you around. Now you are going to die in this miserable cave.'

I am ready to face my ordeal. I believe he will not risk a shot, but I cannot be sure. It is a risk I must take. He does not know what a worthless lot my erstwhile companions are. They might just as well be a thousand miles away for all the good they are to me — but of this he is unaware.

I know the talking is done. I have trekked hundreds of miles for this moment. I must not let it slip away from me. I must stir up his fury, blind him with it so he is no better off than me.

'It is you who are a fool!' I shout at him. 'You know I am too good for you. You're just a killer with no brain. You're worse than a wild animal! That's why you're hiding in this cave.'

He snarls with anger, but I give him no rest. 'You deserve the fate of all those poor people you've sent to their graves, but wherever you are, their spirits will come back to haunt you. There'll never be any rest for you, Escobedo, in this world or the next! You . . . '

I hear his angry intake of breath and know my tirade has snapped his patience — as I intend.

The stomp of his footfall sounds on the rocky floor. He is far closer than I fear. As I stumble to the side, I fling up my arms and feel the cracking impact of his rifle-butt. I grab at it immediately, disregarding the pain, my hands locking on to the wooden stock. We struggle, but I wrest the weapon from his grasp, hurling it away. We both fall, each flailing with our fists. He collapses on top of me, winding me, but he is up immediately, cursing wildly in Spanish, telling me that my time has come.

For a moment, the only sound is the

heaving of our breath — and then another sound comes, a gurgling of water. He is gulping water from his canteen. I hear him recork it. I hear him spit.

His laugh comes again, merciless, deadly, hysterical.

'You poor worm!' he screams.

I change my approach. 'All right,' I gasp. 'I was wrong. You are too good for me, but I have money. Look, I'll show it to you!' I plunge my hand into the pocket of my coat.

'You fool,' he cries. 'I'll take whatever you've got anyway.' And then he is on me again, pouncing with the ferocity of a cougar, his snarling lifting to frenzy. His hands are suddenly on my throat, his weight pinning me down as his long-nailed thumbs bite into my wind-pipe.

I wonder if he is surprised at my lack of response, why I do not raise my hands in any attempt, albeit hopeless, to fend him off. Instead, I experience the redness of ebbing life, the pounding in my ears, just as a drowning man does, seeing in my head images of my past . . . James, my father . . . I am walking along the narrowest of ridges. On one side is the chasm of life — but I am beginning to topple the other way . . . the other way, where the fires of hell rise hungrily towards me, their flames like beckoning fingers, licking higher and higher. I hang on for as long as I can, enveloped with the smell, the breath, the physical pressure of my attacker, now as close to smothering me as an unwanted lover — and I sense that I am about to fall, fall . . .

Within my pocket, my index finger seeks desperately for its appointed place within the trigger-guard of the Derringer. The finger seems suddenly stiff and clumsy. I fear it will fail me, but suddenly its flexibility returns and it finds the trigger. I align the thick barrel of the Derringer. Lacking any possibility of missing, I experience a fleeting ecstasy as my grip tightens on the trigger. *This is the moment.*

The detonation is vicious, scorching, escaping from the squeeze of his body against mine. It rings on and on in my ears, reverberating, awakening a great scurrying of bats high in the rock ceiling above. Eventually, I imagine their tiny inaudible voices raised in incredulity. They have not known such disturbance for a thousand years.

Escobedo's strangling grip has slackened; his thumbs no longer dig into my throat. I am gagging, gasping, coughing, drawing air into my burning lungs. His weight is crushing me, forcing my ribcage inwards, suffocating me. I try to heave him away but I cannot. All my strength seems to have departed. I fight the encroaching mists of oblivion.

I lose this battle.

15

I regain consciousness. I know because I feel the pain in my body. I can breathe only in the shallowest of inhalations. I wonder if my lungs have somehow burst and are bleeding. I wonder if my ribs are broken. If I die, I think, it does not matter. What can this world offer now that Becca is dead? High above, the bats have quieted, their brief agitation slipping back in the innate knowledge that they are no longer threatened. I am sick of Escobedo sprawled upon me and decide he would not make the pleasantest of bedmates. My throat is burning. I know that seconds more of his throttling would have finished me. Now, instead, it is he who has perished. I wonder where Jug and Kelvin are. Surely they cannot have missed hearing the crack of the gun from the recesses of the cave. Why have they not come in to investigate? Why have they not rescued me from the crushing weight of this man I have killed? Or perhaps, during my unconsciousness, they came and saw and departed, leaving me. That would fit their characters.

I move my left hand, flex my fingers. My right hand is still imprisoned in my pocket, my index finger curled around the trigger of the Derringer, which is unable to fire another shot until it is recharged. Yet it has served me well. James's killer has paid for his crime, and he will no longer pillage, rob and inflict his terror on other people. The might of his gang has been broken.

But now what?

I move my hips and legs. I feel agonizingly stiff, but inch by inch, I find renewed strength to ease myself from beneath him. Eventually only my left leg is trapped. I am exhausted, and for a while I am obliged to rest. My breathing is now coming in long rasps and I am greatly relieved, for it means my lungs have resumed normal function. Presently, I get to work on my leg. It feels like the heaviest work I have ever undertaken. The limb seems numb and lifeless and finally I am forced to ease my boot off to draw it free.

I force myself into a crouching stand, working my limbs to restore the circulation. After a moment I restore feeling to my left leg. I grope around, retrieve my boot and replace it. I wonder how much time has elapsed since I entered the cave.

Again the question looms in my mind. Now what?

It occurs to me that I have no future here. I must escape from this cave. Can I again expect the recurrence of the miracle that had my horse waiting for me, justifying his name? I cannot believe that such amazing luck will be repeated. But for a moment it seems that it is the only hope I have, my only chance of survival. I must therefore retrace my steps to the cave entrance.

As I step forward, fortune affords me

a favour. My foot kicks something solid and, stooping down, I discover my stick. Thus armed, I grope my way along. I am afraid that I may be going deeper into the cave, instead of towards the entrance. But soon my reaching hands find familiar extrusions from the rock wall and I grunt with satisfaction. I try to proceed by the same route as I had earlier followed, but in reverse. My pace is slow, but at last I feel warm air touch my face and I hear the call of birds and realize I am standing in the yawning hole which is the entrance.

I cup my hands to my mouth and in the loudest voice I can muster, I shout: 'Jug! Escobedo is dead. All is safe now!'

I strain my ears for their acknowledgement, for the sound of their boots rushing across the rocks, their incredulous acceptance of the stark fact that I, despite my disability, have overcome our enemy. Perhaps they may even afford me a pat on the back.

But there is no response.

I repeat my shout, but the reaction is

just as soul-destroying. Not a murmur. Not even the neigh of my faithful beast.

I slump down. I have never felt more alone. Not even the voices of James or Becca probe into my mind to offer guidance.

The pain in my throat is throbbing. I know it is badly bruised from his terrible grip. I raise my hands to it, try to massage away the hurt, but it is useless. The inside of my throat feels as dry as a parched desert. I need water. I could grope around for days and not find any. But I know that people who die of thirst are usually those who succumb to panic. I close my eyes, force myself to think.

I recall one of Escobedo's last actions — to drink from his canteen. I must find that canteen. I was foolish. I should have found it before I made my way to the cave entrance. Now I am determined to retrieve the water.

I am growing quite familiar with my route along the cave wall, knowing that it offers no insurmountable obstacles.

Ten minutes after turning back, my hands search the ground beside the Mexican's body and gratefully grip onto the canteen. I sup from it, holding the water in my throat, feeling its soothing coolness. I restrain myself from drinking too much. I must conserve it, for there is no telling when next I will find water. I am recorking the canteen when the sound comes, causing my neck-hair to rise.

And as I crouch, frozen with the realization that another being has discovered me, a recollection hovers in my mind. A fact that I have not considered since Louis Dupont spoke those words after the canyon massacre of Escobedo's gang. *Escobedo got away. He and one other, riding a single horse.*

Fool that I am! I have forgotten his companion.

The sound is repeated, but I realize that it is not an aggressive sound, not a sound that indicates that somebody is about to inflict violence upon me. It is a groaning sound, human surely, but not threatening.

'Who is there?' I demand huskily.

The sound again. It seems to beckon me. On my hands and knees I feel my way across the cave floor, encountering small rocks and other obstructions, and the sound grows louder. It is feminine and it is desperate.

I find her in what seems to be a small alcove in the cave wall. I feel her dress, her heaving body, the bonds that bind her hands and feet, and finally the bandanna that is drawn tight across her mouth. I struggle with the tight knot, eventually loosen it and pull the bandanna away from her face.

'Who are you?' I gasp.

She does not answer. Her breathing comes like the panting of a dog. I loosen the bonds on her hands and feet.

'Who are you?' I repeat, and she gives me the answer my soul is crying out for, her voice nothing more than a rasping whisper.

'I am Gabriella Carleton.' Even in its

weakness, I recognize her Louisiana drawl.

'And I am Raoul Webster,' I say. 'I was on the coach when it was ambushed.'

'Ah . . . the blind man.'

'Yes,' I confirm, 'the blind man. I am here to rescue you, to take you back to your father.'

'Oh God,' she sobs. 'Thank you, God.'

After the remaining bonds are removed from her ankles and wrists, she is able to stand up, but she is very uncertain on her feet and she clings to me for support. There hardly seems any weight to her. I suspect that she is greatly emaciated, far different from the radiant young lady on the coach. I do not question her about her ordeal, about how she escaped from Escobedo. How she survived whilst free. How she was eventually trapped once more. I do not ask her about the abuse she has suffered at the hands of cruel men. I know that I will hear about it in due course.

'Escobedo,' she whispers. 'Where is he?'

'He is dead. I shot him.'

'I am glad,' she says, and her tone is hard, almost triumphant. 'I am so glad!'

'Can you walk?' I ask.

'I think so, but I feel very stiff. Escobedo kept me tied up for many hours.'

'I shall have to rely on your eyes,' I say. 'I will need you to guide me.'

'I will do it,' she says.

'Firstly then,' I tell her, 'we must get out of this cave. We will have many difficulties after that, but we must take it in easy stages.'

I retrieve the canteen and my stick, then we proceed slowly towards the cave entrance. She hobbles badly. She has suffered much. I cannot promise her instant salvation. The future is like a curtain concealing either life or death. But I have a guide, and Gabriella has the first inkling of possible freedom. It is a good start.

At the cave entrance we stand for a moment, feeling the warmth of sunshine.

It is now that Jug calls my name: 'Webster!'

He is quite close.

'Why didn't you come when I called last time?' I ask.

'We figured it was some sort of trap, that Escobedo probably had a gun in your back. We reckoned he'd shoot us down as soon as we showed ourselves.'

I did not respond.

'Now we've got to get ourselves out of this god-forsaken country,' he says. 'The sooner we get the girl back to her father, the better.'

'And the sooner we get our wages paid the better,' Kelvin adds.

I am never to see Patience again. He must become another memory. I can only pray that he is blessed with a new owner who treats him with the kindness he deserves.

* * *

It is 1906, and twenty years since I returned Gabriella Carleton to her grateful father in San Francisco. My own father died shortly after I got back. He never recovered from the loss of James. He left me his not inconsiderable wealth and the grand house in which I live here in Albany.

The scars inside my head remain but have softened with time.

I have grown used to my blindness. I have made a successful transition and do not feel blindness is a liability. I no longer fight it, but embrace it. It has become part of my being. I would miss it were it not there, and suspect that an explosion of light into my eyes would be a frightening and unwelcome intrusion. Indeed, I doubt I could handle it, for I would become too aware of the world's imperfections. Now, it is up to me what I make of it in my mind. I can create it as a heaven or a hell, depending on my mood, which I generally pride myself as being positive. And there is the question of my face. I have forgotten what it looks like. I am sure a reflection in a mirror would not be pleasing.

Studying the incredible system invented by Louis Braille, I have become proficient at 'reading' with my fingertips. My life is full and I enjoy it.

I have become a writer of fiction and poetry of the great American West, striving to tell the truth about the frontier during the brief time I was able to observe it. It was not a bit like the penny-dreadfuls that flood the markets today. My writing may lack visual impact, but I believe the wisdom and foresight I have acquired are the secrets of its success. Anyway, I once heard somebody say that the past gets stuck on the back of a man's eyelids, and that is true. My work has been compared favourably with that of Mark Twain, Bret Harte and Owen Wister. I am fortunate to have a very good secretary, to whom I dictate my work, and a supportive editor.

Gokliya and most of his following survived the attack by the *rurales* on the night Becca and I escaped, but he subsequently surrendered to General Nelson Miles and was incarcerated for a time in Florida. On his release, he lived at Fort Sill, where he became something of a tourist attraction, selling pictures of himself for twenty-five cents. For fifty cents he would sign them in block letters. Of all things, he recently took part in the inauguration parade of President Theodore Roosevelt, riding in the Washington procession as if he was the nation's greatest hero. Now, however, I have heard that he is drinking so heavily that he will shortly be destined for the grave.

The Indian wars of the South-west are over, but peace has been bought at great cost — the lives of many whites, military and civilian as well as Apache. And there will always be a stain of dishonour across our nation's history.

Perhaps, before Gokliya's demise, I will visit him and see if he can solve the mystery of Becca. How she became part of his band, where she appeared from, why she could not speak Spanish, despite the fact that her knowledge of the Mexican terrain was profound. Alternatively, I may never enquire, but allow the past to sink into obscurity. I will form in my mind, like so many other things, my own version of her story.

I have only recently picked up the courage to relate my experiences in Mexico. For a long while, my memories of Becca have created personal sentiments in my heart, which I did not wish to share, but now I hope the time is right, for her kindness and selfless fortitude are worthy of recording. She was the light of my life, the star by which I have spent my days. Eventually, I know, we will be reunited. Meanwhile, I am determined to take advantage of the fact that I survived that dark and violent time in Mexico and the South-west, a survival that Becca, in no small part, helped me to achieve.

We do hope that you have enjoyed reading this large print book.

Did you know that all of our titles are available for purchase?

We publish a wide range of high quality large print books including:
**Romances, Mysteries, Classics
General Fiction
Non Fiction and Westerns**

Special interest titles available in large print are:
**The Little Oxford Dictionary
Music Book, Song Book
Hymn Book, Service Book**

Also available from us courtesy of Oxford University Press:
**Young Readers' Dictionary
(large print edition)
Young Readers' Thesaurus
(large print edition)**

For further information or a free brochure, please contact us at:
**Ulverscroft Large Print Books Ltd.,
The Green, Bradgate Road, Anstey,
Leicester, LE7 7FU, England.
Tel:** (00 44) **0116 236 4325**
Fax: (00 44) **0116 234 0205**

Other titles in the
Linford Western Library:

A TOWN CALLED TROUBLESOME

John Dyson

Matt Matthews had carved his ranch out of the wild Wyoming frontier. But he had his troubles. The big blow of '86 was catastrophic, with dead beeves littering the plains, and the oncoming winter presaged worse. On top of this, a gang of desperadoes had moved into the Snake River valley, killing, raping and rustling. All Matt can do is to take on the killers single-handed. But will he escape the hail of lead?

THE WIND WAGON

Troy Howard

Sheriff Al Corning was as tough as they came and with his four seasoned deputies he kept the peace in Laramie — at least until the squatters came. To fend off starvation, the settlers took some cattle off the cowmen, including Jonas Lefler. A hard, unforgiving man, Lefler retaliated with lynchings. Things got worse when one of the squatters revealed he was a former Texas lawman — and no mean shooter. Could Sheriff Corning prevent further bloodshed?